ROLLER DERBY VAMPIRE

THANK Y
FOR YOUR
SUPPORT!
JOSH BLACKMON

ROLLER DERBY VAMPIRE GIRL

THANK YOU FOR YOUR SUPPORT!
Josh Blackmar

ROLLER DERBY VAMPIRE GIRL

Josh Blackmon

ROLLER DERBY VAMPIRE GIRL

Copyright © 2020 Josh Blackmon

All rights reserved.

ISBN: 9798552342891

DEDICATION

For my wife, Emily, and my daughter Olivia.
Thank you for being my biggest fans and support system.

And to Antonia, the original Roller Derby Vampire Girl

ROLLER DERBY VAMPIRE GIRL

ACKNOWLEDGMENTS

A special thank you to everyone who supported me along the way. All the friends who put up with me talking about this for a decade and those willing to read it multiple times to try and help bring my dream to paper.

And thank you to my parents, who growing up, always encouraged my creative endeavors, no matter how weird they were.

ROLLER DERBY VAMPIRE GIRL

Chapter One

Masters Of Our Own Demise

The trouble for Greg began on a Thursday night. Well, truthfully, the trouble began for Greg in his sophomore year of high school. He secured a position on the varsity football team, and life changed for him. The pride of small town America. It would take Greg years to overcome the damage that high school sports culture had unknowingly caused him. In the small bubble that is high school, he was a god among boys. Ever so slowly and innocently, his personality was consumed and confused. His identity became the sport—it was what he did, who he was. He was the pick of the litter. He was a football player and nothing more. He didn't *have* to be anything more than that.

Post-high school had been a rude awakening, and he was still recovering. He worked on regaining the person he was before he became little more than a game. He was often accused of being short-tempered, a stereotypical jock. He knew he was more than that. He knew he had more to offer, but he struggled to remember what it was he used to offer society that would make people like him. He just wanted people to like him. He missed the adoration and the attention. Greg had discovered one thing that temporarily afforded him the praise and approval he was chasing. His reliance on it would be his undoing.

While sitting alone in his dark bedroom, blackout curtains tightly drawn, slightly drunk and festering in a muggy cloud of dank herbal residue, he found himself bathed in the glow of carnal swiping. A digital buffet of skin and loneliness at his disposal. And at the moment, he was embraced by feeling utterly alone. Sound judgment was not on his side. Desperation took the reins. It would be a fatal mistake.

Greg was no stranger to window shopping on hook-up apps. He typically chickened out at the last minute. He did fairly well for himself bar hopping most weekends, but he was high and horny and ready to make a few bad decisions. He switched around the filters on the app and sorted it by distance. He quickly swiped past a few photos he recognized and knew would be dead ends. And then he saw her. The little green notification that she was online and under five miles away perked up his spirits and his penis. Overlooking the ease and high probability that he was being catfished, he sent a direct message to the raven-haired vixen.

This girl most certainly wasn't from the area. He definitely would've remembered her. Her photos were clearly an impromptu shoot for the app. They may have been taken that same day. She must have been as hard up as he was. Or at least that's what he hoped. The photos were all regrettably cropped to meet the app's often skirted nudity standards. *No tits,* he thought, but she definitely wasn't afraid of showing skin. She had one leg thrown up on top of a white wooden vanity, looking over her shoulder wearing knee high leather boots, a black lace thong, and nothing more. *Dirty pictures in her Nana's house,* he laughed to himself.

What's up? he typed swiftly, mouthing the words as he wrote them, certain that this witty greeting would win her over. He pressed send and waited. Much like a watched pot, he had not really expected a response. These apps were a numbers game—put a lot of lines in the water, just hoping for a bite. This one was definitely biting. She responded almost immediately.

In town for a few nights, she replied.

Bored. You?

Each phrase a separate line. Rapid fire.

He watched them come in one by one. He ran his tongue across the back of his teeth and sat up a little, thinking carefully about his next move. Working through the chemical fog he had created in his own mind, he decided to keep it simple.

Same. He hit send and started typing a follow-up immediately. He wasn't sure how long this gift of a woman would be online. She was probably talking to forty other dudes already. His message was bold, but easy to overcome if it was too forward, too soon. *Want some company?*

Nothing.

He had fucked it up. He'd tried to set the hook before she even took the bait. In his impatient frustration, he nearly threw his phone across the room, but before letting go, he felt it buzz. She had replied.

Maybe.

Her reply was loaded and complicated. He had to be careful. If he came on too strong, it could blow the whole thing. But if he didn't send the right signal, she might lose interest. He was calculating all the options when she beat him to the punch, sending a follow-up response.

Pics?

You first, he replied playfully, finishing the request off with a silly smiling emoji.

Greg was a frenzy of excitement, sitting up in his bed, hunched over his phone, and waiting to see if this girl was the real deal. The phone buzzed moments later, and he clicked the image icon to open the attached photo. "Holy shit," he said out loud. This girl *was* the real deal. She was stretched out like she was posing for a renaissance painting or about to solicit some cash from a paid fans account. Her hand, not holding the phone for the photo, was up by her face with her index finger resting resting gently on her bottom ruby red lip, the faintest hint of teeth biting the end of her fingernail.

Now you, she sent shortly after.

This was Greg's time to shine.

He leapt up from his bed, nearly tripping over his game controllers tossed on the floor by his bed. He ran over to his closet and reached in, grabbing his letterman jacket from the back. He threw it on over his bare chest, checked his hair in the mirror at a quick glance, and kicked the boxes of empty fast food containers on the floor out of the way from where he was standing. In his rush to spot clean, he knocked over a cup, sending watered-down sweet tea spilling on the floor. He would worry about that later. He kicked off his boxers and held the camera up and pointed it down, showcasing as much of his body as he could and making sure to highlight his best qualities, his letterman jacket and his well above average dick.

He snapped a couple of photos, and satisfied with the result, sent them immediately.

Seemingly unthwarted by a nearly thirty-year-old man brandishing a high school letterman jacket, she replied, *So you wanna meet up?*

Greg pumped his fists in a silent victory, a celebration to himself.

Sure. Anything more, and he was afraid he would appear as eager in text as he was in real life.

Greg looked around his room and suddenly hoped she wasn't planning on coming here.

You know the liquor store on Cork and Elm? she replied before he could be too worried about it.

For sure, he texted back. *I'm like 10 minutes from that place.*

Cool. I'm staying down the road with some friends, she replied. *Meet me there in 15? We can pick up some drinks and head back to my place. Your treat?* She ended with a winking emoji.

His treat indeed. At this point, he would buy her the whole store.

See you in 15, he replied.

Greg fumbled around the room into a pair of jeans, threw off his jacket, and put on a white thermal long-sleeved shirt before making the call to wear the letterman jacket in an attempt to make it easier for her to spot him. He shoved his feet into a pair of boots and stumbled over the laces to the bathroom, smiling at himself in the mirror and checking his breath by breathing into his hand. He grabbed a bottle of mouthwash and swirled a generous swig then, spit it back into the sink and wiped his mouth with this sleeve. He shoved his phone into his pocket and shut off the lights as he left. It would be the last time Greg would see his apartment. It would be the last stupid decision he would ever make.

Managing to drive himself to the liquor store took less time than it should have as he whipped down the residential roads, ignoring the posted speed limits. Had the police been on their guard, perhaps they would've concerned themselves with his lead foot. Maybe they would've arrested him, and he could've slept it off in the county lockup, but they didn't. Instead, he made his way to the 24-hour liquor store. He saw her waiting outside for him as he pulled into the parking lot. Even in the harsh overhead fluorescents, she was eye catching. He walked over and they awkwardly hugged. She giggled at him. He assumed it was the excitement of the evening, or maybe she had felt his eager manhood smashed by the denim prison of his pant leg. She had instructed him to go in alone. She wanted to be surprised. She kissed him on the cheek and sent him in the store by himself as she waited outside in the cold. He wasted no time browsing—he found the highest proof, fruitiest bottle of cheap liquor he could and was soon heading out the door with a brown paper bag in hand, greeted by the sexy smile of the mysterious woman he had begun a conversation with less than an hour prior. They both walked to his truck, and she climbed in the passenger seat without hesitation, like she had known him forever. No reservations of meeting and hooking up with a stranger.

If Greg had been thinking clearly, maybe he would have begun to see the signs that things were not as they seemed. But even on his best day, Greg still might have missed the red flags.

They pulled into an empty spot along the sidewalk and parked. On the drive, she had mentioned that she and some friends were staying at her grandmother's house while they were wintering in Florida, and if the neighbors saw a strange truck in the driveway, they were likely to call the cops—or worse, her grandmother. They were typical snowbirds by the way she described them. Greg laughed, saying it explained the floral bedspread that looked like it was from the 1980s. His dark haired date laughed and agreed with a nod. There was no accounting for taste she had added, looking at his letterman jacket.

Greg had not caught the joke.

They walked less than a block to the greyish blue little house. She opened the unlocked door and let him into the dark foyer, closing and locking the door behind her. He kicked off his loosely tied boots instinctively and threw his jacket on the back of a chair that he was able to make out as his eyes were adjusting to the room. Then he noticed several other figures in the room.

"Are your friends still awake?" he asked innocently, turning back to his date.

It was the last thing he remembered before coming to with a sickeningly sweet liquid touching his tongue and filling his mouth. He gagged, nearly vomiting. He jerked his head away from something or someone who had him craned upward, encouraging him to drink the liquid. The room was dark, his vision was blurry, and his head was pounding. Greg suddenly realized he couldn't really move his arms or his legs. He recognized the smell of cold, damp steel from his time working in hardware. He was tightly fastened to something. He tried to jerk his body free, but he was chained to something heavy. A woman's voice came from the left, startling Greg. He could only make out blurry shapes, but he was sure it was a woman.

"Who's there?" he practically screamed.

"You need to drink," the voice replied calmly. "You need to keep your strength, keep your energy up." Her voice was sweet, but her message was anything but.

"Where am I?" It was the only other question that he could muster translation from his brain to his mouth. The gravity of his situation was just really beginning to sink in.

"You're at an old warehouse near the shipping yards," she replied calmly. "Now please, drink this."

"Why? What is it?" Greg was angry and scared. "Why am I here?" He was rambling. He wasn't thinking clearly—but how could he have been?

"It's Gatorade," the woman replied with a chuckle, as if it was the dumbest question he could have asked. "The electrolytes help keep you going. It helps keep the blood pumping," she explained with zero restraint or sense of secrecy. "Did you know that a person can lose up to about 30% of their blood before they pass out? And about 40% before they die."

Greg realized how cold he was and began breathing rapidly. A combination of fear and the beginnings of hypothermia. He was still clothed, but they were damp.

"For a guy your size, that would probably be somewhere around one and a half, maybe even two liters." She was explaining it all like you would go over the features of a new car—matter of fact but with good-natured salesmanship. "You seem pretty strong, a former athlete." This was tinged with mocking that Greg now definitely heard. "We could probably push our luck with you. But we never do," she said as she put the bottle back up to his mouth, forcing him to drink. "We're very careful. You last longer if we are."

Greg didn't really comprehend any of what was going on, but he knew it was bad for him. He kept trying to make his mind process what his blood had to do with anything. Where was his date? Was she okay? But he had little time to figure it out. Before he knew it, his caregiver called for the others.

"He's awake, and he's hydrated," her voice echoed in the small, metal room.

Not long after her voice had rattled out of the room, several more women made their way around him, and a flood of light from the outside illuminated what he could now see was some kind of sanitation closet he was being held in.

"Where is—" Greg realized he'd never asked the girl's name. "Where is the girl? Is she okay?"

Greg still didn't get it. He had been set up.

"Where is she?" he cried out forcefully.

One of the women came and stood in front of him.

"I'm right here, baby," his vixen said with a haunting laugh.

Her jet black hair held no warmth, and her features were now harsh and cold. She was gorgeous, but more than that, she was deadly. She leaned forward and placed her hand on his chest, then without warning, she gripped the fabric of his shirt and ripped it from his body in one swift and painful motion. The force from it left a stinging kind of road rash under his arms and around his neck.. It left him even colder and suddenly feeling raw and uncovered. The woman of his digital fantasy, now standing in front of him, took her hands and put them up by her face, licking the tips of her sharply filed fingernails and leaned back in towards Greg. She pressed her icy fingers against his skin just below the collarbone, and before he knew what was transpiring, she dug her nails deep into his skin. Breaking the surface, she held them there, pulling down ever so slightly and agonizingly to encourage the blood to pour from the wounds. Greg screamed out in unspeakable pain as his blood pumped and ran down his chest to his abdomen. Bambi removed her fingernails from his torso, which hurt nearly as much as they did going in. He screamed out again, nearly losing consciousness from the pain. He struggled, but he clung to his sense of living as the dead frenzied around him, licking their lips, enticed by his blood-painted torso.

His attacker stepped back and licked her fingers again, sucking his flesh from her nails. "Watch your teeth, girls," she cautioned. "Make sure you stop them before he's dead. If we play it right, he'll last us a few days. I'm going out for a bit."

The woman who had lured him here turned and left the room. She disappeared, leaving the rest of the vultures in the room to begin licking and sucking the blood from Greg's freshly punctured flesh. Every flick of their tongues or graze of their lips stung like fire, and eventually, Greg lost touch with the world around him—unsure if it was from the pain or the blood loss, but grateful for the relief.

He awoke later, shivering. He looked down, realizing his clothes were gone. The room around him was a dusty yellow. Streaks of light from holes in the wall gave him his first true sense of his prison. For the first time, Greg could see the room where he was destined to die. It was daylight. He could sense the sun. He looked around. He was indeed in some sort of custodial closet. His mouth tasted dry and sickly, and he was frozen to the core. His body shivered uncontrollably. He wasn't sure whether it was from the blood loss or his naked body resting on the concrete floor in the unheated, dark dungeon in the middle of November, but either way, he was struggling to be able to move his toes. He was sure he could still feel them, but barely.

Greg looked down at the dry, blood-caked trails lining his chest and took a deep breath, just now realizing the extent of his injuries. He started trying to move his arms, to somehow break free, but he looked down and saw the thick chains that bound him to the wall. He started crying out of frustration, realizing the desperate place in which he found himself. Out of fear and anger, he began screaming. At first, they were guttural and animalistic, but then he began panicking and yelling—begging for anyone to help him, for someone to please come and save him. But no one can save you if no one can find you. Greg was a lost soul.

The events of the next few evenings repeated like the days before them: excruciating pain gave way to excruciating pain and then numbness. He would black out, coming to every so often. Once, he vaguely remembered his fingers being sliced and nicked and the blood being sucked from them. The last words he heard mocked him. He had apparently pissed his pants during the events of the first night, leaving them no choice but to strip him of the rest of his clothes and dignity. He would remember nothing else. He would wait at the doorstep of death until the beautiful murderer finally came and sank her fangs into his neck, bleeding him dry, and putting him out of his misery.

Chapter Two

Blood in the Heart

The rhythmic clack of the hardened resin plastic hitting the ground with each alternating lunge forward was nearly hypnotic. Regina, better known as "Princess Slayer," wheeled down the barebones hardwood rink. She grabbed the railing and popped over the small step that separated the aging skating rink from the stained indoor/outdoor carpet floor. It was a seamless transition. Elegance in motion.

Her rich mahogany skin glistened with sweat as the cool, sapphire undertones of her completion highlighted her slender, muscular frame. Her coarse curls bounced back into shape as she ruffled her hair with her fingertips.

Some people found their second home in the water. Regina readily, but not regrettably, acknowledged her refusal to conform to societal norms and had never learned to swim. Some people found themselves at home behind the wheel of a car, a true mechanical manifestation of their soul. Regina recklessly drove a 14-year-old foreign hand-me-down with faded bumper stickers and a perpetually cracked windshield. However, when she laced up those jet black roller skates with the bright sunflower yellow wheels, she was no longer a terrestrial slag, she was no mere man—or woman, rather. One foot in front of the other, walking?

Laughable. No, not her. Not this celestial creature.

No, Regina was endowed with a gift of speed. The track was earthbound perfection. She became someone different on the rink, transformed with the armor of those who rode before her. The skates, the gear, the helmet with the little cartoon bumblebee sticker crookedly affixed to the side. Yes, she *was* this Princess Slayer they all spoke of. And in certain circles, they all spoke of her. She was a menace to her foes, a terror to those who dared to cross her, and a heroine to every feminine adrenaline charged member of the Hunny Bees.

She was a derby girl.

Off the rink when the skates came off, and her knee pads were thrown haphazardly into her battle weary gym bag, it was a different story entirely. Like most days post-practice, she was sitting alone at a concession table picking at a plastic tray of nachos, whose cheese had long since grown cold and unappealing. It was in those quiet moments that she was just Regina Reynolds, a 27-year-old black woman living in a rural east coast town, making ends meet and struggling to keep the spark aglow in her eyes that was once so unmistakable. That spark was what drew Grayson to her the first day she laced up a pair of khaki rented roller skates and unceremoniously fumbled her way through the seating area, trying to make her way to the rink.

Grayson Hines was not what you would call a classic underachiever. A better description would be more of a non-achiever. Regina had given him a little, if not too much, credit for simply keeping the doors open at the skating rink. And even she realized that her rationale of being impressed that he had managed to hold down a job while trying to get his big break in the music industry may have been doing more harm than good. Grayson was as tragically unmotivated as he was talented. It was that reality that Regina struggled more and more to shake, desperately trying to ignore. She wanted nothing more than to break the cycle but kept falling back into a pattern that, despite her best intentions, she continued to reinforce.

Beyond his faults and their issues, of which there were many, their love had been enough to cover the glaringly obvious, if unmentioned, problems they both continued to leave unaddressed. Regina had no doubts in her heart that she loved him and that he loved her. Grayson had given her the greatest, most enriching gift of her life: he had taught her to skate. Most days, that was enough. Most days, they made it work. Beyond their genuine feelings for each other, Regina's ego also refused to let their relationship crash and burn. Though it was rarely a topic of conversation, or most days even noticed beyond passing glances at the local Olive Garden, Grayson and Regina were the only committed, long-term interracial couple within a 60-mile radius. She had a vested cultural need to make it work.

Regina had begun to fear though, that for her, "just making it work" wasn't enough.

The microscopic yet consistent fraying of the little loose threads of their relationship was becoming more and more evident. Little fights bubbled and simmered, always threatening to breach the surface. She realized the extent of how much it really wasn't working one Saturday before derby practice. The slow churn of their relationship's dysfunction abruptly rippled to a boiling point.

Regina tossed her bag onto the seat and slid into one of the ratty and faded secondhand restaurant booths by the concession stand then lined up and tightened the velcro straps of her knee pads. She was quickly joined and cordially greeted by two other women who were also making last minute adjustments to their gear before practice. Directly across from her was Veronica, Regina's best friend and confidant.

Veronica was a pale, mousy, girl-next-door type. She *could* be pretty (and was, for all practical purposes), but she did little to highlight her better features—or any of her features, for that matter. In a 90s teen rom-com, she was the girl who took off her glasses and got a makeover, only to become unrecognizably gorgeous . . . but Veronica didn't wear glasses, and she never got that makeover. Often she was the subject of a running joke that her overly prudish image was the result of a strict Amish upbringing. It was a complete fabrication, but the joke had given her great potential for her derby persona, the "Quaker Shaker." The friends were also joined by Regina's younger derby apprentice, Tabitha. Regina and Tabitha were the only two women of color on the otherwise fairly monochromatic team. Tabitha's mother was Puerto Rican, and her father had done little more than contribute to her conception, but his absence never left her for lack of identity. Her warm brassy skin was also an accurate reflection of her personality. She and Regina had bonded immediately and quickly attained play-cousin status. Almost instantly, she was dubbed as the Slayer's protégé. Her low center of gravity and compact frame, bright cateye glasses, and quick reflexes had earned her the moniker of "Tabby Cat." Tabby had even hot glued two little felt ears to her helmet to fully complete her ensemble. Regina saw so much of herself in Tabitha. She was a version of Regina that had every possibility in the world open to her and more importantly the ambition to still chase after it.

As Veronica (who, very true to form, always walked into the rink early, dressed, and ready) unzipped her duffle bag to grab her mouthguard, she shrieked with an ear-piercing but giddy glee. She lightly, frantically tapped her feet on the floor and fanned her hands in excitement. She reached in and pulled out a cheap, store-bought bouquet of flowers just as Grayson walked up with several bottles of water, setting them on the table for the women.

"Is it your anniversary or something?" Grayson asked casually, not really caring, but feigning interest for the sake of keeping the peace between him and Regina. Veronica was one of the few people who still paid him for rink hours when she came in to skate laps. He'd learned to muster a little attentiveness for the life of a returning customer.

Veronica's joyous response that they were "just because" flowers struck an unappealing chord of jealousy in Regina, and she quickly shot a glare directed right at Grayson.

He stared back at her, dead-faced and confused in a way that only Grayson could manage. His gawk ruptured the thin shield that contained Regina's anger.

"Why don't you ever get me anything 'just because'?" she snapped at him with a bite that was definitely less playful than she had heard it in her own head. Self awareness when it came to recognizing the tone of her own voice and inflection was often not at the top of the list of things Regina excelled at.

Quickly deflecting and trying to ever so gently defend himself while still dripping with sarcasm, Grayson graciously motioned to the bottles of water he had just placed on the table. "I brought you these," he said, but not satisfied to leave it at that, he added, "and don't I always give you the cookie from my Lunchables?"

And at that moment, simple as it was, the floodgates opened and the stagnant, festering resentment and white hot anger spilled out in a spectacular and absurd presentation. "And it's like a slap in the face!" Regina spewed. "I like brownies, Grayson. BROWNIES!" She yelled at him, probably even more loudly than she herself had expected to.

To anyone other than the two of them directly involved, this was a childish and ridiculous thing to fight about. And to be clear, it *was* childish and ridiculous—the great cookie versus brownie debacle. To the two of them, it was the representation of every issue they had ever glossed over, every all-night, hours-long fight they had ever had, every relationship crack and fracture they had ever deliberately ignored. Regina had grown tired of Grayson's obvious contentment in their relationship, like in every other aspect of his life. She had grown tired of her *own* contentment. All she wanted was to be more than the mediocre cover band or rundown roller rink in his life. But she wasn't. Regina was finished. She was prepared to walk away over a cookie.

"That's it, we're done," Regina said with the cool, calm, and collected determination of a woman who would most certainly regret what she had said later.

"Okay," he whipped back flatly with a slight scoff and head tilt.

A glorious aura of rage was slowly giving Regina a luminous glow.

"Why aren't you more upset?" Regina scolded, in a stupor that now bordered on the manic.

Grayson was matter-of-fact in his delivery. With a striking lack of enthusiasm or concern, he moronically replied, "Because I know you, Regina. In ten minutes, you'll change your mind, and we'll be like we've always been." And as if that wasn't enough, he topped it off. "So I'm just going to ride this one out."

Regina would have been furious and succumbed to an extravagant meltdown right then and there had she not realized he was absolutely right. That dummy was correct. In their typical fashion, she would explode then cool down. They wouldn't mention the blowup, and neither of them would apologize because neither of them would ever admit that they were wrong. More accurately, neither would ever *think* they were wrong. Regina furrowed her brow as her internal thought process read across her face like braille. It was sinking in. She really was ready to break up with him.

And with a deep breath, Regina found the nerve to grab the hammer and begin to pound away at those final nails, plunging them deep into the coffin of their flatlining relationship.

"Maybe that's the problem," she said, vocalizing her own thought process as she was figuring it all out for herself. "We will be like we've always been." She took a pause that hung in the air like laundry on a stagnant summer afternoon. As she broke the silence, her voice rattled, the drainage from the tears she was holding in collecting at the back of her throat. "I don't want to be like we've always been." A second, far shorter pause—barely enough time for her to second guess the words that followed. "Grayson, this is it."

She held strong, clenching her teeth and calculating her every breath, willing with every ounce of emotional self-abuse to keep the precipitation that was welling up in her eyes from spilling over into tears.

It was only moments earlier that Tabby and Veronica realized they were no longer witnessing one of Regina and Grayson's awkwardly comedic and embarrassing public spats. And both had seen their fair share. No, it had become clear they were now front and center for the actual break-up. The unwitting audience to the dissolution of a six-year relationship. They were trapped in the booth with no way out, caught and forced to watch the train wreck as it ripped loose from the tracks.

Grayson was unquestionably stunned. His dumbfounded acceptance of the situation was growing fearfully angrier by the minute as he discerned the absoluteness of her voice. A real ending to their relationship had not crossed his mind. Not ready to lose her, but nowhere near ready to back down, he forced out the words without thought, "Are you seriously breaking up with me over some flowers?"

"No! I'm breaking up with you because you don't understand that this *isn't* about some stupid flowers," Regina replied sharply as her hurricane of emotions was finally settling into the calm of righteous anger.

"Hey!" Veronica unconsciously chimed in defending her tiny bouquet of day-old, wilted, grocery store daisies and sprigs of green grass. She was more than a little offended they had been called stupid. She clutched the flowers to her chest as if to protect them from the insult.

"Sorry," Regina said instinctually, with genuine sentiments. "I didn't mean it like that."

"You know what?" Grayson finally replied, his tone riddled with forced nonchalance. "You're right, Regina." Grayson puffed out his chest, hoping his body language would mask his true feelings and allow him to salvage some upper hand in the situation. "We are done. I don't have to put up with this, or you. I'm going to work."

Grayson then made his own dramatic display. As he walked away, he aggressively swung the single saloon door by the front counter open then loudly kicked a folding metal chair, sending it skidding across the floor to the opposite end of the counter. He stomped over, sat down, and threw his feet up on the counter. It was then he realized that it would be hard to save face, as he had stormed off a mere twenty-five feet away from his now ex and her friends. But he held strong (as any dumb man can in situations where he was clearly wrong).

Veronica and Tabby remained seated in a state of shock, but they were no more stunned than Regina herself—now knowing beyond a shadow of a doubt with that display, they were really over. Most of their break-ups in the past had led to a little hot and heavy action in the back room, pressed up against the Lysol-scented shelves of rental skates, but there would be no romp around the rink this time. There would be no more romps. There was no more Regina and Grayson.

Regina had steeled herself up for the break-up, but she was not prepared for the finality of being broken-up. She was numb. A voice called to her from the rink, somehow piercing through the haze that was perpetuating around in her brain. She would have to shake it off for now. Right now, it was time to hit the floor. A distracted jammer was a bad jammer. And as cool as it sounded, a bad jammer was not a good thing. Regina willed herself back to reality and skated over to the entrance to the wood floor of the rink, making sure her eyes didn't cross paths with Grayson's, though she could feel his eyes glaring with every click of her skates.

Chapter Three

Aren't We All Suckers . . . For Love

Regina glided gracefully out toward the center of the rink and focused her mind as she crouched into position for the first go-round. She shook her head, the loose straps poking out from under her helmet swatting back and forth like they were working in her favor, trying to brush off the very recent memory of her last fight with Grayson.

Despite the best of intentions, her brain boiled over with anger and pain. The whistle blew, and as if by some power not her own, she flew past the girls, laying several of them out flat as she maneuvered around the pack. In peak form, Regina became a battering ram of female force, leaving destruction in her wake and points on the scoreboard. Coach Ella, a stocky short-haired brunette woman in her forties and the aptly monikered coach of the Hunny Bees, had positioned herself on the wall and was jumping up and down triumphantly, screaming at Regina.

For her entire life, Regina had used her physicality as a cure all for pain. Forcing adrenaline to drown out her mental suffering. Her current outlet was roller derby. In college it had been the crew team when her parents started marriage counseling. Even at nine years old, she ran laps around her backyard until she passed out on the day of her grandmother's funeral. Whether it was because of the breakup, or in spite of it, Regina was having quite possibly the best practice of her career as she tried to outrun her feelings.

The post-practice scene of triumphant back slaps and hugs disintegrated once she arrived back at home. Alone. After leaving the praise of her coach and the cheers of her teammates for a practice worthy of *Sports Illustrated* (if *Sports Illustrated* focused on roller derby), she quietly came in the front door, trying not to wake her roommate who had fallen asleep in front of the TV. Like most nights, derby practice ran long. She was dead to the world, and that was fine with Regina, since she definitely didn't feel like talking. She silently crept down the darkened hall into her bedroom and shut the door behind her.

Regina dropped her bag to the floor. She reached up and grasped the small round handles on the top drawer of her dresser, and as she did, she caught her reflection in the mirror. Regina hadn't realized she was crying. In truth, she'd been crying the entire car ride home. She looked down, trying to escape her own sad reflection as she tugged out an oversized t-shirt from the inexplicably full drawer of nightgowns. As she struggled to push the drawer back into the dresser, she noticed the several small picture frames that were situated on top, each filled with images of herself and Grayson. Each one a memory. The oldest of the photographs was a small strip of four panels taken not long after they had gotten together. They were from the now broken and out of commission photo booth, quarantined in the back storage room of the roller rink.

"Every kid has their own dang photo booth on their cell phone now," Grayson had told her as she helped him push the booth out of sight and out of mind. Sadness makes for a keen keeper of memories. She couldn't help but think about him. And suddenly, she couldn't force herself to remember all the bad. It was like a cruel joke. She stood, tears running down her face, shirt halfway on, and her lycra shorts at her ankles. She was haunted by happiness. Good memories flooded her consciousness, each nearly tangible enough to reach out and touch. The day they met felt like a fresh wound, and it stung.

Regina was fresh out of college, working at the local news station in a new town far from home and putting in her dues until something better came along in the city. At the behest of her mother, she was going to get out of the house and do something. "Anything," was what she had been lovingly instructed to do. The opportunity for recreation had presented itself by fate.

Grabbing the local shopper, which she rolled up tightly with the sole purpose of killing a large wolf spider scampering across her floor, she had swung ineffectively several times, resulting in a frantic spider darting directionless and trying to escape. Without time to regroup and swing again, the spider (with all eight of his hairy, spindly legs) disappeared somewhere among the piles of clothes, moving boxes, or worse yet, beneath the bed. At that point, this meant the room itself basically became a war zone. The bed, a casualty.

"It is impossible to sleep knowing a spider is waiting for you," she had said to herself.

Shopper still in hand, she grabbed a wooden chair from the kitchen and sat with her back to the door, cross-legged and watching the floor, waiting for the spider to reemerge from his foxhole. The wait afforded her the time and boredom to actually look through the shopper. Her original intention for even picking up a free copy of the swap meet style publication was to rewrap some vases she had unpacked then decided to donate to a local secondhand store. It was there sitting in that little chair, perched and waiting for a spider, that she had seen the small ad. Nestled amongst the larger, more colorful and flashy ads, it was simple—clean black type against a white background with a thin little border around it.

FREE SKATE LESSONS

The price point was unbeatable, so she decided to heed her mother's urging and get out, maybe even meet someone. And meet someone she had.

A few days after seeing the swapper ad, Regina found herself walking through the smudgy glass door of the roller rink. The rink was outdated even then. It smelled old, but in a charming way, like the allure of a library without the sense of knowledge and literacy. At two in the afternoon on a Saturday, it was also practically deserted.

Regina walked up to the counter where a young man stood with his back turned to her. She waited briefly, as patience was a foreign concept and was only magnified by the fact that despite her best effort, she was still really nervous about the whole excursion. Regina cleared her throat to get his attention, then immediately saw the little metal service bell and worried she would die of embarrassment. He turned around, almost startled. He smiled at her—it was a goofy, genuine smile that was accentuated by his short, bouncy curls and stubble speckled face. It wasn't quite a five o'clock shadow, but maybe like a three fifteen shadow. Either way, It made that crooked grin of his seem to go on forever and it caused his blue eyes to flicker playfully.

"Shoe size?" he asked her casually.

She replied, "Nine," with a small grin. She couldn't ignore that he was cute. Not the kind of guy she would ever actually date, she thought to herself. Unkempt, wrinkled concert tee, probably in a band, claims to love the Ramones, huge fan of Wes Anderson films. She knew the type. But there was definitely no harm in looking.

He turned around and went to the back to grab the skates and quickly returned, resting the worn and beaten rentals on the counter.

"Four-fifty," he said nicely, maybe a little too nicely. Regina was feeling more relaxed every moment. This boy was definitely flirting with her. It took the edge off a little, being somewhere new and unfamiliar.

Regina reached in her bag, pulled out several crinkled dollar bills, fumbled together some change, and placed it on the counter. She hoped in her mind the interaction had gone more smoothly on her side than it seemed. Not that she was flirting back, but she wanted to hold her own. She took the skates with a smile and sat on a nearby bench to wait for the rest of the class to arrive, her knees bouncing with anxious, nervous energy as she kept nonchalantly looking around. The brief relaxation she had felt with the skate clerk had faded.

There was no one else showing up. Had she gotten the wrong day? As many times as she looked at that ad while mulling over the decision to actually come, had she gotten the date wrong? That was the only explanation for her solitary position at the roller rink. She now felt sel-conscious, the blood rushing to her face. Regina resigned herself to embarrassment, stood up, went back up to the counter, and put the skates down. They clammered together, making a louder noise than she had hoped. The young man turned around and lifted his eyebrow with a quizzical grin.

"I think I changed my mind," she managed to get out—super casually, no tinge of awkward energy, she thought, strangely propping one elbow on the counter then putting it back down almost immediately.

He smiled, no worse for wear. Thank goodness he hadn't noticed. "Okay, let me get you your money," he paused. "Can I ask why?"

No, dear Lord, just let me leave with some of my dignity, she thought.

"I think I have the wrong day," she admitted.

"How so?" he replied, propping his elbows on the counter. "Never a bad day for skating," he added, slightly grimacing at his own comment.

She relaxed a little. "I saw this ad in the shopper for free skate lessons, but I have the wrong day." Regina clarified, overexplaining the predicament she had found herself in.

"Why do you think it's the wrong day?" he asked, now having a little fun with her.

"I'm the only one here," she countered back with a Vanna White gesture to the empty room, showing a little of her trademark wit.

"I can assure you that most of my classes are this poorly attended." He grinned. "I'm Grayson. Why don't you come and sit back down, and I'll help you lace up your skates?" he said, jumping over the counter, already wearing skates and wheeling her over to the bench.

She felt a flutter of energy as he brushed the tip of his fingers on the back of her arm, guiding her to the sitting area by the concessions booth. Regina sat back down, and Grayson knelt down in front of her. Before she could stop him, he took off her shoes and set them to the side. Regina was overcome with embarrassment as this strange guy was down on the floor messing with her feet. At the same time, there was something really romantic about it, and now that he was up close, he smelled so much better than she expected—like clean linen. She quickly reminded herself of her rule when it came to cute guys that she knew were wrong for her or that she knew she would have no real future with. *Look, but do not touch. Do not engage—for the love of God, Regina, please don't.*

"Have you ever skated before?" he asked, making conversation as he readjusted the laces on her right skate. She didn't realize that she was wearing Hello Kitty socks until she got back home that evening, a moment of true agony that still would wake her from a dead sleep some nights.

"At a birthday party about fifteen years ago, and I pretty much clung to the rail," she began to nervously ramble. "To be honest, I never really thought about skating until I saw your ad, and then I remembered that movie *Whip It*—have you seen it? It had that pregnant girl from *Juno* who is all political now. It's pretty good, and I thought, to myself 'Hey, self, you might really like roller derby.'"

"Oh yeah," Grayson said, halfway paying attention to her, but mostly distracted by her shapely bare legs. "Okay, hop up, and see how those feel."

Regina stood up, a little wobbly as Grayson led her, clomping (not unlike a mechanical horse) as she teetered her way through the concession area to the rink. She stepped off the short step and almost immediately tasted hardwood face-first, but Grayson caught her before she hit the floor. He held her upright, and she braced herself against him. He smiled, and she looked up at him and couldn't help but smile back. Regina stood back up and Grayson slid his hands down to her hips, beginning to guide her around the rink.

Early on in their passes around the rink, she kept her hands spread out for balance like a wobbly eagle. But as she became more comfortable, she took her hands and placed them on top of Grayson's, and their fingers lightly interlocked. Regina had broken her rule. The warm strength in his hands was invigorating. At one point, he spun her around, and they were looking eye to eye. He smiled at her. It was all over.

Now she sat alone in her room, alone in the world, looking at pictures. Perfect memories replayed on repeat. She would never meet another Grayson. Regina realized she would probably never have that moment of magic in meeting someone like that ever again. Those kinds of things were once in a lifetime. She'd wasted hers on Grayson. She lay on her bed, forgoing her plans to shower and instead cried herself to sleep.

Chapter Four
And Then She Appeared

The week post-break-up had gone by slowly. She hadn't spoken to Grayson since that night at the rink. He had texted her nine and a half times. She counted the half as the time when she could see that he was typing then stopped. *It counted.* She hadn't responded to any of his attempts, but she had watched each message come through. Read the words. Memorized them. Heard them in her head as she imagined the tone of his voice as he would have said them aloud. "Are you still mad?" "Are YOU still mad?" "ARE you still mad?" Tonight would be the first night that she would be forced to see him in person. The picture frames were easy to turn over, but Regina had never considered before how often circumstance would dictate that she run into her ex—once, sometimes twice a week at practices, home bouts, team parties. This would not be easy. Regina willed herself to power through because this was something that was going to happen. She was eventually going to have to see him sooner or later, and she might as well make it now. She cared more about derby than she cared about her own pettiness. *Mostly.*

When she got to the rink that night, she quickly walked past the counter. Regina was grateful Grayson had been distracted enough not to notice her, or at least not to acknowledge if he had noticed her. She sat down and began to gear up. She'd never spent more time lacing up her skates, fixating on them with her head down so as not to risk accidentally meeting eyes with Grayson. Veronica and Tabby arrived not long after Regina, and it eased some of the nervous tension that plagued Regina's body. But it wasn't anxiety like she had expected or braced herself for. For the entirety of the drive over, the fear in her mind was that the skating rink she loved so much would now be awkward and tarnished because of him, painted with memories too hard to overcome. Instead, the feeling that she kept struggling to try and fight off was the feeling of wanting him back. Woefully missing their late Sunday morning walks or quietly singing along as he played on the guitar. More than anything, she wanted to rip that stupid thrift store concert tee right off, right over his head, take him into the storage room, and have her way with him. He must have been rearranging the store room or cleaning the toilets with the way the sweat was glistening on his arms. Had he been working out? This was the opposite of how she thought she would feel. The nagging feeling she'd been pushing away all week—she'd never let the thought grow to more than a momentary lapse of judgement, and now she had no choice but to confront it. She realized she might actually miss Grayson.

"Are you wearing makeup?" Veronica asked, caught off guard by the obvious addition of mascara and the faint hint of shimmery gold eyeshadow to Regina's usually minimal practice palette.

"Did I make a terrible mistake by breaking up with him?" Regina blurted out unprovoked, having not even heard Veronica's comment about her makeup.

Tabby nodded her head vehemently in affirmation, almost rocking the glasses from her face. For as much as she loved Regina and Grayson together, she was more convinced that both of them were too socially stunted and stubborn to ever find other suitable matches. They were perfect for each other because no one else would ever put up with their nonsense.

Veronica shot a scolding glance over to Tabby and proceeded to reassure Regina, "No, you didn't." She squatted down to meet Regina at eye-level. "As sad as we all are that you guys split up, it was for the best." Then the mother-hen in her wrapped it up with a nice little well-meaning bow. "You both deserve to be happy, and clearly that was no longer possible with each other."

Regina halfheartedly nodded in agreement. The thought itself was comforting enough. She did deserve to be happy. She just needed some time. Time to get over him. Time to let herself let him go. She had all intentions of marrying that man one day. *Feelings don't just go away,* she told herself. "You're right, I can't expect myself to get over it in just a week."

Unfortunately for Regina, any comforting thought was about to escape out the door like an opportunistic latchkey kitty as the raven-haired mystery vixen walked in the door of the rink. She was gothically, hard rock stunning, her long jet black hair in loose curls that caught the breeze from the circulating fan whirring back and forth on the countertop. It lightly lifted and bounced around her shoulders—the scene wouldn't have been out of place in a shampoo commercial. She wore a black leather jacket snuggly wrapped over a simple white tank top that stopped just short of the waist of her minuscule jean cutoff shorts. Her knee high, matching leather boots made a muffled but unignorable clacking as the thin heels struck the floor. It was her own personal applause for the parade she led as she made her way to the counter, where she had now caught Grayson's attention, as well as Regina's.

She watched as the normally unconcerned and unkempt Grayson took the extra steps of running his hands along the waistband of his jeans to tuck in his tee shirt and combed his fingers through his hair giving it an effortless sense of polish.

"Who is this bitch?" she blurted out. A fit of possessive jealousy oozed as the words erupted from Regina's mouth probably louder than they should've or she even realized. An unbiased recognition of her own volume level was not one of Regina's marked traits. She blamed it on hearing problems which she did not have, truthfully she was just unapologetically passionate. Veronica and Tabby both turned around in their seats to see what had gotten her so worked up, and they were equally impressed. The girl had a presence, and it was magnetic. Her appeal was undeniable.

Tipping her head down and glancing over the rim of her glasses, Tabby said, "Wow, those are some *short* shorts." Her accurate observation only got Regina even more riled up.

"Those are not shorts," Regina was quick to correct her. "Those are denim underwear." Regina was livid. "Unacceptable. It is November! Who even wears shorts in November?" She was approaching a dangerous point of anger where words sharpened and slid right through her already damaged verbal filter.

"I kind of like it," Tabitha admitted. "It's a look."

Veronica unwittingly stirred the pot even further as she added, "She seems awfully flirty with Grayson."

At this point, Regina no longer saw colors or heard sounds—she was blinded with rage. She no longer needed all five senses, and the nonessentials were replaced with anger. "I'm going to kill her. And then I'm going to kill him!" Regina said, too consumed with the situation to even gracefully get up out of the booth.

Tabitha, the youthful voice of wisdom, interjected at probably the wrong time—with definitely the wrong words of encouragement, "You know, you broke up with him."

The slow and purposed turn of Regina's head as she looked Tabitha in the eyes to reply to her was otherworldly. "Eight days ago!" She rattled on, "Just because I broke up with him doesn't mean I want to see him happy. Especially before me! He should still be in mourning at this point," Regina uttered.

Tabitha doubled down on her characteristically astute observations of how the situation was presenting itself at the counter, and the situation was presenting herself quite clearly. "He doesn't really look all that mournful to me."

"Thank you, Tabitha," Regina responded with dagger eyes. "When I need you to tell me things that I can see with my own eyes, I'll let you know. Okay." No one was now immune to Regina's fire.

Trying to lighten the mood, Veronica foolishly thought that somehow her next words would've offered any kind of help. "She is kind of pretty though," she said with a sweet smile.

Veronica was not a great mood lightener.

"Yeah, if you like trashy pale groupie chic," Regina said. "It's called the sun girl. Ever heard of it?" Regina spoke rather loudly now, nearly loud enough for the subject of the conversation to be able to hear it. "That round bright thing up in the sky. . ." she trailed off.

Veronica scolded her like a child talking in church. Regina tried to retort, but at that time, the woman was walking out the door, and Grayson was on his way over, "All I'm saying—oh, she's leaving!" Regina was frantic, "Oh, he's coming over here. Quick, act like I said something funny. No, like we're mad at him—no wait, funny."

Regina erupted into a loud and clearly fake laugh. Veronica and Tabitha stared at her in bewilderment. "I'm funny," Regina said as if it was the entirety of an anecdote no one had asked for. Grayson gave her a look as he came to a stop right in front of the table. He had slowed as he walked up though, and the pep in his step to have an excuse to talk to Regina was tempered when he remembered that he and Regina were no longer together. He wasn't even really sure if they were friends anymore. He decided not to let it get the better of him.

"Did you guys just see that girl up at the counter that I was talking to?" he asked, not yet realizing the conversation he had walked into.

Regina whipped back, slinging malevolence, "Every little nook and cranny."

Grayson eased out a sigh of relief. Honestly, Regina was easier to deal with when she was mad. He would take angry Regina over sad Regina any day. Mad covered sad. "You know you may want to consider a dress code here," Regina suggested. "I'm just saying. I wouldn't want her to catch a cold—and die."

Grayson ignored her tone and continued. He had interesting news and didn't plan on wasting it. "She's a derby girl."

"Oh no! And our team is all full. What a shame," Regina dramatically faked disappointment. "Well, she can go across the train tracks and be a cougar. She looks more like a cougar anyway. Her skin looked old," she said touching her eyes gently and nodding at Tabitha, silently encouraging her to agree. Regina was on a roll.

"She actually has her own team," Grayson explained. "They reserved the rink tomorrow night and paid up front, even the deposit—no one ever pays the deposit."

By this point, Grayson could sense the pleasantries of their conversation were evaporating quickly, and he buckled up and settled in for the ride. He was ready to bicker with Regina. That he was good at. That, they were both good at. Grayson once referred to arguing as their "kink" Regina had taken offense to it, which started an argument.

"There's a new derby team in town?" Veronica asked, genuinely curious about the prospect of new competition.

"Yeah. The Hunny Bees better watch their backs," Grayson said half-jokingly.

Regina scoffed at the thought of a new team being any competition for the well-oiled machine that was the Hunny Bees.

"I don't know," he said. "Scoff all you want, but she seemed pretty hardcore. She showed me some videos on her phone—the Bloody Mother Suckers seem pretty legit."

Veronica was taken aback by the name that could be easily fumbled by the tongue into an obscenity. "Is that their name? Really?" she asked. "That is borderline offensive."

Tabitha chimed in, "I've never heard of them. Are they registered in our region?"

"I don't think so," Grayson answered, not certain. "It seemed like they were part of some kind of traveling league. Bambi did say they travel a lot."

Grayson knew her name, Grayson had remembered her name, and Regina had to respond quickly with something biting and mocking. "Bambi? Oh my God! That's her real name?"

Regina's wit had not served her as well as she hoped. She could have done better.

Grayson had reached the limit of what he was ready to take without retaliation and had been eagerly awaiting for this moment. He was preparing to tear it wide open and finish it. "Yeah," he said with a smug grin and head tilt, "and she signed it with a little heart over the 'i.'"

Grayson wasn't really known for being an asshole, but he knew how to turn on that obnoxiously cocky tone, and today he did so with great ease. "Right before she wrote her phone number underneath it." He smirked, knowing he had hit her at her core. He walked away, leaving Regina with her mouth agape and fighting back the tears welling up in her eyes.

Chapter Five

People Start Disappearing

Regina grabbed her bag off the floor, dragging herself out of the booth and stormed out of the rink. She refused to let Grayson see her cry. As soon as the door swung closed behind her, she urgently picked up her pace, approaching a near sprint. Regina quickly reached her car and fumbled with her keys to no avail. She threw them to the ground and let herself sink down onto the damp asphalt of the parking lot, leaning her back up against the driver's side door.

Hidden in the shadows away from the flickering street light, away from the rink, she let herself cry. Head buried in her hands, poise abandoned.

Thankfully, it wasn't long before her personal pity party was interrupted by Veronica and Tabitha. Veronica sat down next to Regina and put her arm around her, pulling her in tight to her chest. She cradled Regina like a child who had fallen from their bike and scraped their knee. Tabitha crouched in front of them and dabbed the tears from Regina's face with the bottom of the sleeve of her hoodie. She had been wearing mascara, and it was now running all down her face.

"Can you believe him?" Regina mocked Grayson through her tears. "'Right before she wrote her number underneath it.' I hate him."

Tabitha tried to control her facial reaction. Hating him wasn't what caused this outburst.

"He's just trying to make you jealous," Veronica said, trying to comfort her.

"Well, it's working!" Regina said, needlessly stating the obvious. "Look at me!" she said as she sat back up and motioned to the mess she was at the moment. Clearly, it was working. She was sitting on the ground crying in a dark parking lot. It was not one of her proudest moments.

"Really, Regina?" Tabitha said with a little tough love. "It's Grayson—what are the chances he'll even call her? He's not the most go get em' guy."

She hadn't really meant any genuine offense toward him, but Tabitha doubted that Grayson had the follow-through for sudoku, let alone pursuing this woman who was, simply put, miles out of his league.

"Chances are pretty damn good," Regina replied. "Did you see her? Hell, I would probably call her," Regina joked, poking a little fun at herself. But she was right—even Regina wasn't immune to the facts—Bambi was gorgeous. She was sad, she was definitely mad, but Regina wasn't blind. Regina had ro real reason to hate her other than she was now encroaching on two things that Regina still thought of as hers. Roller derby and Grayson. Neither of which she was ready to let go.

Veronica seized an opportunity and tried again to ease the situation, "I don't know," she said optimistically. "We've known Grayson a long time, and I just don't think Grayson would be like that. That girl was just so overtly obvious with her sexuality."

"Yeah, 'cause guys hate that," Tabitha chuckled out sarcastically.

"See, Tabby Cat knows what I'm talking about," Regina said clinging to the support of her wallowing. "He's probably having sex with her right now." No sooner than the words exited Regina's mouth, she began to cry again. Simply thinking of him with someone else tore her up inside. She was not over this boy in the least.

Almost as if on cue, waiting in the wings, Grayson came running out the door, calling over to them, "Hey, hold up, don't leave!"

"Wow, that was quick—not saying a lot about Grayson's stamina," Tabitha whipped out. "Poor Bambi."

The understated sex joke caught even Veronica off guard and gave her a laugh. Normally, she would frown upon that kind of cheap humor, but she couldn't help but laughing a little at Grayson's expense. And he deserved a little of it, the way he was behaving around Regina, flaunting his flirtation with Bambi.

Regina quickly dried her eyes, grateful for the cover of night and the harsh streetlight shadows. Hopefully, he wouldn't notice she had been crying. It wasn't even so much a concern, as Grayson seemed fretfully distracted, like someone had walked in on him in the bathroom. His deer in the headlight eyes and slightly flushed cheeks gave him away with what could only be described as a subdued panic. Tabitha was right, he couldn't even muster the gumption to be panicked at 100%. He half-assed everything.

"Hey, you guys haven't heard from Greg, have you?" he asked, a little short of breath from his jog over. "Why are you on the ground?"

"I—" Regina stammered, quickly cut off by Veronica.

"She dropped her keys under the car. We can't reach them," she said as she gently pushed the keys with her hand underneath the car.

Tabitha mentally tagged herself in, jumping in to help take the focus off Regina. "Greg with glasses or Greg without?"

It had been a long standing tradition amongst their tight-knit group of friends to refer to the two Gregs as Greg with glasses and Greg without. This was despite the fact that Greg with glasses had gotten laser eye surgery and had not actually needed glasses for nearly three years. The nickname was not one that he could not escape. After all, their group already had a Greg without glasses.

"Greg without—no one has heard from him in over a week." Grayson's voice was more serious than the girls had expected. "Jerry and Orbache talked to his folks a few minutes ago. They are filing a missing person's report." Grayson sounded worried, and his tone left no room for misinterpretation. The gravity of the situation was well understood.

Veronica's heart fluttered, jarred by her pulse racing with the thought that something could have happened to him. She had briefly had a crush on Greg some years ago—a childish crush that had long since faded the more she had gotten to know him, she was worried nevertheless.

"Isn't he sort of flaky like that though?" Tabitha asked, bringing up a valid point. Greg would often go days without calling anyone. During college, he was known for pulling all-nighters then sleeping for hours on end, dead to the world missing phone calls and texts, even once sleeping though someone banging on his door. Lately, it was usually just managing a hangover after a reckless night, but he'd always turn up.

"Yeah, but never like this. He hasn't shown up to his job. His voicemail is full, he hasn't returned texts in days, no social media." Grayson said solemnly. "To be honest, even I'm a little bit worried." And it was obvious that he was indeed concerned.

Regina couldn't help herself, and the words came out of her mouth like vomit—uncontrollable and unharnessed. "Maybe Bambi can help you find him."

"Really?!" Grayson said, genuinely a little upset with the lack of Regina's respect for the situation. "You know, you broke up with me! Are you regretting it? Is that what this is about?" Grayson had enough of the lingering break-up politics. He hadn't wanted to lose her, but right now he didn't want her back.

Tabitha once again nodded her head. Regina did want him back—she hated that he wasn't hers anymore. "If you love something, set it free" was a concept that she did not subscribe to. Regina bitterly regretted cutting Grayson's leash and now she was too stubborn to try and chase after him. Instead, she would now tear him down until he wanted her back, or she would break him down so much that she could convince herself that she no longer wanted him. She wasn't proud of it.

"No! I just can't believe you would go from me to someone like that." Regina spat the words at him.

"You know what, Regina, I wasn't going to call her," Grayson admitted. This admission came as no shock to Tabby. "To be honest, she scared me a little. But I am going to now. And I am going to take her to dinner. At Red Lobster."

Grayson could play her games, too—fights between them had always run like well-rehearsed stage reading of immaturity. Each had their cues, and there was no curtain to close. But they both had a clear mission: hurt the other as much as possible. Thus, Grayson had now invoked Red Lobster. *Their* Red Lobster.

"That is our place!" Even Regina had not expected him to go as far as to take this new girl to their place. So much romance had transpired surrounding the golden cheddar biscuits and endless lobster platters. He had first told her that he loved her at that Red Lobster. It was sacred.

They had gone to dinner at the Lobster that night, like they had so many times before. It wasn't a special occasion; to be honest, the evening was wearing thin on Regina. A child near them had been loudly making noises and screaming the entire meal, and Regina assumed the child's parents must be deaf or stupid to allow such behavior to continue. There had been zero attempts to silence their screeching banshee child. At one point, Regina had crept over to the lobster tank and pulled one from its watery glass slaughterhouse and made it dance toward the child from behind the wooden partition. The child screamed one final time out of primal fear and for the rest of the night, sat silently watching and waiting for the ghost lobster's return. Grayson was still laughing when Regina sat back down and began drying her hands on her napkin.

It was during that laugh that he freely uttered those three small words that had once held so much meaning. "I love you."

It had turned the entire evening around. She had loved him too. And she couldn't ignore the fact that she still loved him, no matter how much it hurt, or how inconvenient it was.

"Not anymore," Grayson said plainly. "Veronica, Tabby—if you guys see Greg, give me a call please." Then he added, as if it were a fire in his mouth, a curse he had to release with hate and ire, "Goodnight, Regina."

Grayson walked away. He was getting really good at walking away—he had to. He couldn't let her see the pain that it caused him to be so hateful to her. But he had no idea how to deal with the situation otherwise. He wouldn't back down to her. They were both far too stubborn for their own good. But tonight, he was furious with her. He walked back into the rink and joined two guys who sat drinking beer behind the counter. Orbache and Jerry both typically spent their free evenings at the rink, drinking free beer, and unsuccessfully hitting on derby girls.

Jerry was a proud product of the good ol' boy mentality—a nice guy, but not a thinker. He worked at his father's construction business and often smelled of paint and drywall. He was the friend in high school you knew you'd never see again after graduation, but somehow had managed to cling onto them well into adulthood.

On the other hand, James Orenthall Bachman III, better known as Orbache, was a dusty blonde, clean-cut, trust fund kid. Town royalty. His great grandfather owned a small lumber mill, and his father and grandfather had built a textile empire. Despite his pedigree, he and Grayson had met in grade school and had decided to be underachievers together—only Orbache had the plush expense account to actually afford to do nothing.

Grayson let out an angry, aspirated grunt, directed at no one in particular. "Why? Why?" Grayson was fuming as he slammed the cap of a beer bottle on the edge of the table, sending it flying backward. He took a swig from the bottle and forcefully planted it back on the table.

"You know what you need to do?" Orbache was about to offer some sage advice.

"Some dumb grand romantic gesture to win her back?" Grayson hated the thought.

"No!" Orbache replied, dumbfounded. That was the furthest thought from Orenthall's mind. "You need to come out with me and Jerry—a little smoke, *a lot* of drinking. You know, just until you forget her!" So, maybe sage advice wasn't exactly what he was offering up.

"I don't know, I'm not really in the mood." Grayson just wanted to finish his flat roller rink beer, cool his temper, and go to bed.

"And that, my friend, is exactly why it is of the utmost importance that you get drunk tonight." There was no chance that Orbache was going to take no for an answer.

Jerry chimed in, revealing his matted down hair as he removed his Farber and Sons Construction trucker hat and holding it over his heart in comedic reverence and southern drawl, "Drown your sorrows, my brother."

Grayson reluctantly agreed. "Okay, maybe just a few drinks." The thought of forgetting his troubles at the moment did sound appealing if he was being honest with himself. He didn't want to forget Regina, or maybe he did. But he desperately wanted to forget how much he had just hurt her.

Orbache was up and out of his chair, grabbing Grayson's shoulder. "That's what I'm talking about." The night was young, and Orbache's limitless bank account was ready to wash the memory of his best friend's failed relationship away with house liquor. As soon as the derby girls got out of there, they would close up shop and descend upon the town. It would be glorious.

Chapter Six

Just Cover Your Neck (And Your Heart)

The local bar was loud and crowded, filled to the gills with local university students enjoying the precious few weeks before finals. The music was a mix of 90s classics in between live, awful local bands. Grayson sat near the back with Orbache and Jerry and a short blonde girl who had at some point in the evening sat down and joined the group without invitation. As she nursed her Blue Moon, she swore up and down that she remembered seeing Grayson's band play a house party three years ago. She kept suggesting that he get up and sing each time like the idea had suddenly just occurred to her. Grayson probably seemed like a complete jerk to her—not that she noticed. He hadn't really heard two words she had said since her initial greeting. He ignored her to what should have been a painfully embarrassing degree. He just sat and drank shot after shot of cheap tequila trying to forget the terrible things he had said to Regina. His stomach began to churn with an undesirable ratio of much booze to little food. As the hours ticked on and Orbache and Jerry showed no signs of slowing, the awful acoustic love songs and chitter-chatter of drunken coeds finally got to Grayson, and he excused himself and went outside.

The cold night air was a welcome refresher. His face was hot, his lips numb, his eyes were heavy. He could smell and taste the soured alcohol in his sinuses. He thought for a moment he might get sick, but he took a deep breath, and the urge passed. He pulled out his phone and let autocorrect coherently translate his jumbled message to Orbache that he was leaving and going home. But before he went to put his phone back in his pocket, he scrolled down to a saved text hanging out several lines below the one he'd just sent. It was to Regina. His finger hovered over the screen, wanting nothing more than to tap it, open the text, and read the message he had sent her two weeks ago before he went to sleep—just telling her how pretty she looked. The screen went black. The energy-saving function was on a timer and had grown impatient with Grayson. He shoved the phone in his pocket and began to shuffle down the sidewalk.

Shortly after Grayson had left the girls in the parking lot at the roller rink, Regina had been struck with a similar epiphany to drown her sorrows. She had stopped off at the local grocery on the way home and picked up several bottles of wine. Tangled up in blankets, Regina was kneeling on her bed singing into the nearly empty bottle like it was a fun dispensing microphone. Veronica sat on the floor watching the surprisingly entertaining performance. For her, it was somewhere between incredibly funny and desperately heartbreaking. Usually, the song Regina crooned helped dictate the scenario. Her own personal soundtrack. Currently, she was doing a masterfully crafted medley of "Nothing Compares" and "I Will Always Love You." This was one of the times when Veronica was merely an observer—she knew her friend, and she knew that right now it was just important to be here and be supportive. Tabitha had gone home early, having an exam on Monday that she had not yet begun to study for. Plus, at twenty-one, Tabitha couldn't be expected to fully comprehend the complex emotions going on. Regina and Veronica had now moved on from the "I hate him" and "wasted years of her life" to the "women don't hit their prime until forty." Now, the suggestions were part emotion but mostly the wine. The singing stopped abruptly, and Regina sat up in her bed and looked over at Veronica, quite determined.

"You what, what I'm going to do?" Regina said, pointing at herself, puppeted by the wine. "I'm going to get a tattoo right in the center of my left butt cheek. He'd hate that. And do you know what it's going to say? 'Not Grayson's.'" Regina smiled drunkenly waiting for acknowledgement of her great idea.

"That's kind of trashy," Veronica responded with a grimace. It wasn't kind of trashy. Veronica was being polite. It was a terrible idea.

Regina, compromising, offered, "Maybe I'll get like one word on each titty?"

"That's not—that's so much worse," Veronica laughed. She was actually grateful that Tabby wasn't there to hear this string of bad ideas. She might have actually encouraged them. Veronica shuddered and rolled her eyes with disgust at the lowbrow relationship revenge tactic of tattooing.

Regina melted back into the pale lavender comforter bunched up on the bed and pointed the nearly empty bottle of wine at Veronica, gesturing as if to offer her some. Veronica shook her head and held up the small glass of wine she had poured herself from the first bottle, back when at least one of them was still using a glass for their wine. Regina shrugged and poured a bit of the remaining wine into her mouth, and began singing a new song, one that Veronica was fairly certain Regina was making up on the spot, but so far the chorus was actually pretty catchy. She'd had no idea so much rhymed with 'Grayson sucks.' Drunk Regina was turning out to be somewhat of a lyricist.

Back on the other side of town, Grayson was slowly making his way down the street, and despite his inebriated state, he began to sense that he might not be alone. He turned and looked behind him, but the movement had been a little too swift, and his eyes were having trouble adjusting.

"Sort of late for a stroll, don't you think?" A woman's voice came from the darkness somewhere behind Grayson. It was friendly, unthreatening.

He turned around again and this time was able to make out the shape. It was a shape that had left a lasting impression.

"Bambi?" he asked, not sure whether the alcohol was playing tricks with his vision the way it was playing tricks with his feet and occasional gag reflex.

"You look like you could use some help," Bambi offered in a surprisingly sweet voice. It was vastly different than her tough exterior would have led one to expect.

Grayson tried to pull it together, sobering up and not letting on how embarrassingly intoxicated he was, but it was useless. He finally gave up and shrugged with his goofy smile. "I might be a little bit drunk," he laughed, humbled.

"I can see that," she smiled and laughed.

"I'm really embarrassed you are seeing me like this," he said, genuinely wishing he hadn't run into her anywhere remotely close to his current condition. He tried to explain or at least provide context for his situation. "I don't normally drink like this. I swear. I just—," he paused and then just laid it all out on the table. "I just recently got dumped, so my idiot friends took me out to get trashed."

There was something so sincere and painful in his voice that made it nearly impossible not to see him as a droopy-eyed pound puppy.

"Mission accomplished?" Bambi asked, grinning at Grayson. Her words fluttered around him.

Grayson chuckled, "Definitely." He wasn't sure, but Grayson was beginning to get the impression that she was flirting with him.

"Which way is home?" she asked, "I'll walk you."

She was most certainly flirting with him.

Grayson sort of pointed in an ambiguous direction. Honestly, he'd just left the bar and started walking. "I think if I keep going this way . . ." he trailed off.

"Wow, you *are* drunk," she flatly, but then added, "and adorable." Bambi smiled at him and licked her lips as she sort of giggled.

"Yeah—wait. What?" Grayson was caught off guard. She was moving on quickly from mere flirting. She was actually coming on to him.

"Look, some of the girls and I are crashing at a friend's house like three blocks over," she said, clearly laying the groundwork for a proposition. "I needed shampoo, and this town has a regrettable lack of stores open after 10 pm." She held up a plastic gas station bag with a bottle of shampoo in it. "I don't normally do this, and it's probably really dumb, but why don't you walk me home and come sleep it off at my friend's place?"

She held out her free hand to him.

Grayson was a little unsure. The scenario was already a bit of a blur, and he was pretty drunk. His decision-making processes were not at their peak. "I don't know," he finally told her.

She smiled, shaking her head like you would at a child who had just said something absurd. "Well, I can't leave you out here." She smiled sweetly. "If you got run over by a truck or something, I would feel really terrible. Come on, don't put that on my conscience."

"Well, I don't want to get run over by a truck," Grayson said, conceding.

Bambi grabbed his hand. "Can I just say one thing?" she continued without waiting for a response. "The girl who dumped you is missing out."

Grayson shook his head, "She's, she's—"

He honestly had no idea how to finish that sentence. He closed his eyes and his head dipped a little still struggling with his lack of sobriety. His eyes darted back and forth under his eyelids like he was scanning or searching for an answer. His heart had sought out to defend her, but his brain refused, and it had left his mouth with a lack of words.

Grayson looked back up at her. Defeated and empty handed.

This was all the opening that Bambi needed to move into position.

Bambi pulled Grayson towards her, put her arm around him, and rubbed his arm, attempting to try and warm him up. They began to walk down the sidewalk in the opposite direction. Her hand left his arm and crept up his shoulder until it made its way up to his head and she ran her fingers through his hair. The soft-touch was hypnotic enough for Grayson to completely let down his guard.

The next morning hit Grayson like a ton of bricks. The sunlight from the thin curtains hurt his eyes. He went to roll over to face away from the window until he realized he had no idea where he was. He sat up in the bed in a fog. He blinked hard several times, trying to adjust his eyes—willing them to focus. Bits of the evening started flickering in and out. He remembered the bar, he remembered leaving the bar, and he suddenly remembered Bambi.

"Bambi," he whispered with a groggy voice. "Bambi," he repeated slightly louder. Even that minimal effort caused his head to pound. She was nowhere to be seen in the room. Grayson glanced down at the floor and saw his shoes and socks tossed carelessly next to his inside-out pants. It was only in the moment that Grayson became infinitely aware that he was naked underneath the cheap floral sheets of a stranger's bed. He buried his head in his hands.

"Oh fuck."

He rolled over, forced himself out of bed, and grabbed his pants. Pulling his phone out of his pocket, he looked at the time. It was a quarter till eleven. He maneuvered his boxers from the twisted pant leg and began dressing. He had fifteen minutes to get to the rink—he had no time to find Bambi and thank her for taking care of him. The wording in his head sounded all wrong. For helping him home, or whatever. He didn't have time to think about it. He would talk to her tonight and find out exactly what happened, and she would clear it all up. The details for Grayson were muddy, but he had a fairly good idea of the evening's activities.

Chapter Seven

Don't We All Have Fangs?

The thud of an empty wine bottle sliding from its cocoon of blankets and hitting the carpeted floor stirred Regina awake somewhere in the early afternoon on Saturday. She looked down and saw Veronica curled up at the foot of her bed. Her loose and disheveled pigtails sort of reminded Regina of a prissy cocker spaniel. Regina nudged her awake with her foot.

"Wake up," Regina loudly whispered as she tried to encourage Veronica from her slumber.

Veronica stretched, having been curled up much of the night for warmth. "What time is it?"

"Grayson said that bitch Bambi and her team are practicing tonight, right?" Regina asked, completely ignoring the question about the time.

"Yeah, why?" Veronica now realized that she had been awakened simply for this exchange. She rubbed her eyes free of overnight clingers, combed her fingers through her unbraided pigtails, then pulled her hair into a fresh ponytail.

"She may have taken Grayson from me—" Regina started, but was quickly interrupted by Veronica.

"She didn't take him from you." Veronica's tone almost pleaded with Regina to stop creating this competition. Honestly, at this point, Grayson wasn't worth the heartache.

"Well, she's not going to take roller derby away from me. We're going to crash their practice. I want to see what I'm up against." Regina wasn't asking or suggesting—this was apparently the new plan for the evening. "We'll get decked out in black and sneak in there. How good could they possibly be?"

Veronica looked at Regina, knowing she had no choice but to join in on this ill-conceived plan. However, she would be lying if she said she wasn't curious about the other team. Veronica, like a lot of derby girls, had fallen into it by chance, but she fell hard.

At one juncture early in her career, Veronica had taken a writing job at a short-lived, local magazine, *"The Chaos."* The zine, as it was hiply referred to at the time, was focused on fringe sports and alternative lifestyles. She and the magazine had not been a good fit by any stretch of the imagination, but she had needed the job. However, during her brief tenure in chaos, she was assigned a story about a local roller derby team. The other writers, all of whom were men, had pushed it off on her as it was a "lady sport." She was honestly just happy to have an assignment where she wasn't interviewing a testosterone crazed 16-year-old skateboarder or a roided-out high school football player who looked every minute of forty. Veronica hated nothing more than being called 'dude.' Of course, dude was hardly the worst thing she was called. She had absolutely hated that job.

The one bright spot of it all had begun the night she went to interview the team captain of the Hunny Bees. Veronica saw this woman gliding towards her with so much grace and poise, that it was like dance in a strange way. Veronica thought the woman couldn't have been much older than herself, but she seemed to have it all together. Powerful and cool, she was inspiring. That was the night she had met Regina.

They hit it off in the interview. Grayson, who at the time was sort of a local celebrity, had even made her put on skates, go out, and roll around a little with the team while snapping a few pictures for her to take back to the magazine. The concept of scoring and gameplay was phenomenally difficult to fully grasp, but she had fallen in love with the game right then and there. She was a derby girl in an instant. She and Regina had become best friends, and best friends stood by each other.

Veronica sighed, "What time do we leave?"

The night swept in quickly, leaving the sobering daylight hours in its wake. Regina and Veronica sat outside a small house just off campus of the local college. They were dressed in black and would have easily been mistaken for prowlers. A light flicked on at the small front stoop of the house, and Tabitha came running out, waving a quick goodbye to her roommates as she left. She ran up to the car and hopped in the backseat, sliding to the middle and poking her head in between the driver and passenger seat, eye-to-eye with Regina and Veronica.

"Okay, so what's this big secret plan? Are we going to key Grayson's car or something?" she excitedly asked, with the exuberance of a child on their way to the county fair.

Veronica quickly squelched, "NO!" She was shocked that such a thing had even come to her mind.

"Could we do that though?" Regina said, genuinely asking Veronica if it were a possibility. Regina was pretty sure that would make her feel better.

"No!" Veronica said forcefully, reiterating her earlier appall. "We're going to go crash the…" she paused, the words felt awkward and obscene in her mouth, "the Bloody Mother Suckers' practice."

"Why are we all dressed in black then?" Tabitha asked. "You realize there are lights in the roller rink."

Tabitha, ever the voice of reason, and realizer of the obvious.

Regina and Veronica both looked at each other, realizing that Tabitha was absolutely correct. Somehow the idea of dressing in black, sneaking in incognito had made much more sense that morning. Now, it just felt a little silly thinking they could sneak into a well-lit building. Regina shrugged it off and started the car, peeling out of the parking spot next to the curb and nearly sideswiping a bank of mailboxes.

She brushed that off, too.

When they reached the roller rink, Regina took a deep breath and got out of the car. She marched with full force towards the door, shoulders back, head up, chest out, and for a second Veronica saw in her what she had seen the first day she met her—an unstoppable force. Regina swung open the door, and the three women walked in like they owned the place. They were stopped in their tracks.

On the hardwood swirled a bevy of gothic clones.

Tabitha leaned over to Regina. "Okay, good call on the black," she whispered.

Violent didn't even begin to describe the brutality that they were witnessing. Each one of them dressed in black with black hair, heavy black eyeliner, and pale skin. So pale. It was like Bambi had raided an Edgar Allan Poe fan club to put together her team. But Regina had to hand it to them, they were good. Really good. Fearless and violent, like pain was a foreign concept. A girl had just been thrown to the ground and bolted back up, with a bloody road rash burn from scraping the floor and just kept going.

"What are you guys doing here?" Grayson, just now noticing them, asked from the counter where he was propped up, watching the unrestrained massacre.

About that time, Bambi also noticed the trio. They were easy to spot. She snapped at two other girls, Madeline and Victoria, to get their attention. Victoria was a brute, a solid mass of muscle. Her braided black pigtails fell at her broad shoulders. Madeline, a smaller Wednesday Addams looking girl, dropped out of the rank and followed Bambi. They skated over, hopping out of the rink and stopped directly in front of Regina.

"Sorry, girls. Closed practice. We've got the rink reserved tonight," Bambi smiled and said with the faintest inflection of a bitchy high school cheer captain. "Right, Grayson?"

Grayson shifted awkwardly and quietly replied, "Right."

With that, Madeline and Victoria broke away from Bambi, where they had been flanking her, arms crossed. They skated over and began circling Tabitha, who was more confused than afraid.

"Oh, we like her," Madeline said. The words were pleasant, the tone unsettling, and the intent sent a chill down her spine. This girl was creepy. And now as she was circling like a shark, Tabitha was starting to get really uncomfortable. Something didn't feel right.

"Yeah, well we like her, too," Regina said, stepping in the path of the girls and gently pulling Tabitha in the middle of her and Veronica. "In a much less creepy way. She's on our team, so hands-off."

"Oh, you play?" Bambi asked condescendingly.

"We're on the Hunny Bees," Regina said as if none of that needed explaining. "I don't know if *you* saw the big banner on the wall over there, but—pardon the pun but we're sort of the bee's knees around here," Regina said, proud of her pun and pleased that she was holding her own.

Bambi whipped back, "That was probably just until you had some real competition."

Madeline and Victoria made their way back to either side of Bambi, once again crossing their arms and giving the girls a menacing glare, for the first time revealing their uncharacteristically pink, feminine matching string bracelets.

"Why don't you busy bees buzz off?" Bambi said, with no love lost. "We're not recruiting, and we definitely don't need any looky loos, so . . ." Bambi had grown tired of the interaction and was ready for them to leave as she gestured towards the door.

Regina was going to leave. She wasn't going to cause a scene—that wasn't her plan. Causing a scene was usually in her playbook, but not tonight. Regina was going to get the last word though. "Come on, girls," she said. "We're not wearing nearly enough black eyeliner to be here anyway."

They turned in unison, pleased with the outcome of the near altercation. As they were leaving, Madeline whispered something in Bambi's ear and smiled. Tabitha turned her head back to the girls, swearing that she had heard her name. Madeline winked and blew a kiss, and her kiss of death, black lipstick did nothing to make the scene any less ominous.

Veronica grabbed Tabitha's arm and began leading her to the door. The move was instinctive, trying to strangely showcase a motherly possession over her. Veronica refused to look back at them. They just needed to get out the door, and they could figure out the rest later. She selfishly wanted to be as far away from those girls as she could.

They waited until they were in the parking lot before they began going crazy with post-exchange adrenaline.

"Can you believe that?" Regina threw out, stunned.

"How creepy are they?" Veronica added, not usually one to judge, but if the shoe fit.

Tabitha, still a little unnerved, said, "She blew me a kiss."

"I know I say this about a lot of people, but I really don't like them," Regina said.

The door behind them swung open. Regina braced herself and threw her hands up into an awkward fighter's stance, ready for a brawl. She'd seen fights on TV, she was pretty sure she could throw a punch if she had to. Grayson came out of the door. Regina relaxed her aggressive posture, but she was now tense for a whole different reason. Something was wrong, though—it read all over Grayson's face. The door shut behind him, and he rushed over to them.

"You guys need to go home," he said plainly.

"Look, we left the rink. Tell your girlfriend she didn't rent the parking lot, okay?" Regina said, turning away from him, annoyed that Grayson had taken Bambi's side back in the rink.

"They found Greg." Grayson's tone was clear. It was not good news.

Veronica asked, already knowing the answer, "It's not good, is it?" Intuitively, she probed, "Is he okay?"

"No." Grayson shook his head with a certain finality that was readily understood. "It's bad, it's really bad. You guys just need to get home." He was almost pleading. "You don't need to be hanging out in a parking lot at night. Go home, guys. Please." The way he asked, there was something in his voice that let them all know his request for them to leave was sincere. Even Regina held her tongue. When she started to speak, she stopped, understanding enough about the situation to know that now was not the time.

"We'll go. Thank you, Grayson," Veronica said as she motioned for the girls to get in the car. The car ride home was mostly silent. They dropped Tabitha off outside her house, and the car pulled away as she made her way up the sidewalk.

Tabitha was still visibly shaken when she fumbled in her purse to grab her keys. The events of the night weighed heavily on her. Regina and Veronica had offered to stay with her, but Tabitha encouraged them to leave. She'd rather deal with her emotions on her own. Not only was she shaken, but she was also feeling guilty that she couldn't focus on the loss of a friend because all she could think of was what happened at the rink. The standoff, the whisper, the weird kiss. Tabitha had a feeling about all of it that she just couldn't shake. She finally got the door unlocked and stepped into the dark house, frantically closing and quickly locking the door behind her. A sliver of blue light from a cloud-covered moon offered no illumination, and her eyes were struggling to adjust.

"Hello?" *Have the girls all gone out?* she thought to herself. She hoped.

But they almost always leave a light on. It was too dark. Something was wrong. Something was terribly wrong. She scrambled and began groping the wall for the light switch, struggling to catch her breath. Her chest was heavy—a panic attack was setting in. She couldn't find the switch, and in that frenzy, she swore she heard a rustling near her in the room. She stopped. She stopped moving. She stopped breathing. Tabitha tried desperately to let her eyes adapt to the dark, holding her breath listening intently to everything going on around her, but unable to hear anything over the pounding of her own beating heart. Tabitha was now certain she was not alone in the room though. She took a step backward as quietly as she could and slid her hand across the door, reaching for the handle. And then for Tabitha, in an instant, it all went dark.

Her solid frame hit the floor with a muffled thud. Her limp body dragged across the floor. Her hand was still outstretched, lifelessly grasping for help.

Chapter Eight

Did You Hear About Greg?

The next day found a somber, impromptu memorial at the roller rink. Orbache and Jerry were laying waste to a very expensive bottle of brandy from the Bachman private reserves in honor of their fallen comrade. Grayson needlessly wiped down the tables in the concession area, trying to ignore the sinking feeling in his gut he'd not been able to shake for the last few days. The rink had been regrettably as dead as their friend all morning. The moment of silent reflection was broken as Regina and Veronica entered the rink.

"You guys hear about Greg?" Orbache asked as the pair came closer, tossing their practice gear down on one of Grayson's freshly wiped tables.

"Grayson told us last night," Veronica replied with a quiet disbelief. "What happened?"

"Some really weird shit," Orbache answered. "Like, really weird." It was almost as if he still couldn't fully comprehend it himself, but it was combined with the slight hint of morbid fascination.

Jerry chimed in, even less thoughtful and far more bluntly, "I heard he was mangled," excited to be a valued part of the conversation. "By some kind of animal." He paused briefly, trying to decide whether he was going to reveal his next bit of juicy gossip, but he couldn't help himself. "My cousin was the one that drove the body to the funeral home, and he said he looked like the embalmers would have an easy go of it."

"What do you mean?" Veronica asked as if she had uttered that phrase to him a million times, completely unsure of what Jerry was trying to say. Despite the unusual topic of conversation, this was a fairly normal occurrence.

Jerry's eyes lit up with the opportunity to clarify with his own translation. "I mean he was drained."

"Drained?" Veronica asked, hoping she had simply misunderstood again.

"Bone dry. Mummified," Orbache emphasized. The way he had said it sent a shiver down Veronica's spine.

"Exsanguination," Jerry added with a nod, showing off what he held as an impressive vocabulary term picked up from years of taxidermied hunting trophies. "My best guess," he continued with some degree of undeserved confidence, "we are dealing with a vampire." He offered an honest opinion of what he had deduced from the situation.

"That's your best guess?" Regina asked sarcastically. "That's why you're an idiot."

Veronica wasn't going to stand for the bickering and name calling with this. Regina and Grayson's nonsense was taxing enough—this was too much. "Please don't start!" Veronica was begging for a little decorum. "One of our friends is dead."

"Yeah. Regina, we all know you're just raging cause that new derby team has got it out for you," Orbache scolded.

Regina was caught off guard. While she staunchly believed that there was an unspoken war between her and Bambi, even Regina was aware that most of this existed only in her mind. The fact that other people knew about the rivalry was new information. "Says who?" she asked, yet to be fully aware of the reach of the new derby girl and her team.

"Says your banner over there," Orbache said, motioning to the large defaced Hunny Bee banner on the wall. Regina and Veronica turned to see that on top of their beloved and adorably illustrated mascot, Betty Bee, a large black fly swatter had been drawn. Scrawled underneath was the signature of the culprit: "The Bloody Mother Suckers."

"Oh no!" Veronica exclaimed as she and Regina ran over to the sign. Regina reached her two fingers up, and ran them across the signature, and the soft black material smudged. She turned to Veronica with fire in her eyes.

"Black eyeliner." Regina revealed as if she were Sherlock Holmes himself. "It was them all right." She could barely speak.

Veronica yelled across the rink at Grayson. Her voice dripped of anger and sadness. "How could you let them do this?" Her hurt was evident.

Grayson crossed over to them, refusing to yell across the room, "I swear, I didn't see it until I got back this morning to open up for a.m. senior skate." Even in her rage, Veronica could tell he was being honest. Grayson was a lot of things, but malicious wasn't one of them.

A wave of new emotions was flooding every fiber of Veronica. "This is unacceptable!" she uttered, stomping down her foot. "You do not deface our banner—not in my house. This is an act of war!"

"When are they practicing again?" Regina asked Grayson forcefully. It was clear by her tone that leaving this question unanswered was not an option.

"They don't have the rink reserved again until next week, but—" Grayson stopped himself mid-sentence, realizing he had said too much already. Any further, and he feared he would be putting them in danger. But it was too late.

"But what?" Regina had no time for games. She was going to get the information she wanted, and she was going to get it right then and there.

What happened next would years later be one of the moments that plagued the what ifs of Grayson's consciousness. It would be a decision he would feel so much guilt for revealing. It was the split second that would change the course of all of their lives forever. "I did overhear them talk about practicing at the old warehouse tomorrow night," he said apprehensively, immediately seeking self repentance for having said anything at all.

"Those girls are in for a rude surprise," Regina said, walking past him and already heading for the door.

"Wait," Grayson said with a stern force behind the command, following behind her as they both reached the concession area, still walking towards the door.

Orbache laughed, "If she's this upset about the banner, imagine how pissed she's going to be when she finds out you slept with her."

Immediately realizing the present company and the fact he had said this aloud, his eyes went wide.

Regina's feet turned to cement, affixed to the floor. She was stopped in her tracks. Silence fell over all of them in what seemed like an awkward eternity.

"You slept with her?" Regina broke the silence, inexplicably calm.

Grayson said nothing, he just stared back at her. Her beautiful face, her deep soulful eyes that he could now see filling with tears, her lips pursed to hide the quivering emotion trying to escape from them. Regina turned away from him. Hate filled her body. She exhaled the remaining bits of oxygen in her lungs, replacing it with pure adrenaline and bitterness. She grabbed Veronica's arm and pulled her along out the door. Veronica just looked back at Grayson and shook her head in disbelief.

Hearing footsteps behind him, Grayson turned and grabbed the collar of Orbache's jacket as he came up behind him to apologize. The red plastic cup in Orbache's hand went flying to the ground, bouncing and spilling liquid through its trail. Grayson wanted to hit him, and Orbache knew he deserved it, but Grayson just let out a frustrated grunt and pushed him, nearly causing Orbache to fall into the booth and onto the floor. Grayson ignored this and ran out the door behind girls. He caught up to Regina just as she was reaching her car.

"Stop! Stop! Please don't go there tonight!" He was nearly begging.

"Don't you speak to me," Regina angrily choked out through the lump in her throat.

"Beside the fact that you are a total scummy asshole," Veronica said, not even remotely ashamed of her outburst of language, "you let them defile our bee." She was furious with Grayson now as well. For his part in all of it. For hurting Regina, for hurting their team.

Grayson was now literally pleading, "I know, I'm sorry. But you have to listen to me. These aren't normal girls." He was trying to impress upon them the dire nature of his words, but the sentiment fell short.

In a blind cacophony of emotion, Regina heard this statement as praise, not in the least how it was intended. "I don't want to hear a word about her! How could you sleep with her, with ANYONE? We *just* broke up!" she yelled back at him. "I don't care if she is some kind of extraordinary girl."

Grayson was now forced to cover his tracks, trying to make her understand, while also trying to save face. Once again, he knew Regina was not aware of the full gravity of the situation. "That's not what I mean, Regina." Grayson was starting to get emotional, but like a pubescent preteen, his feelings were wild and uneven, and he did his best to shut them down as he argued for forgiveness. "I was drunk—please just listen to me. I saw things last night. These are not normal women." He spoke with every ounce of sincerity he could muster. "Please don't go out there tonight."

"You're right," Regina whipped back. "They're not normal. They're rude, pale bitches who need to be taught a lesson," she barrelled on with barely a breath to carry her through. "You have no right to ever ask me to do anything ever again. I don't even know you anymore." Regina was beyond hurt. Grayson had found the very last button Regina had left, and he hadn't merely pressed it, he had destroyed it. A self destruct code had been triggered.

Grayson continued, refusing to not at least be heard. He was still angry with her, but more with himself, and most of all he was furious with this shit storm of a position he now found himself in. "Oh my God, Regina—I'm serious." His voice was loud, bordering on a yell, but pitched up and tinged with desperation. "I saw some crazy stuff last night. They are brutal! I think they are involved in some sort of fight club or underground roller derby competition. These aren't regular derby girls. Please don't get yourself involved in this."

"Look, you know what? I don't care if Bambi is your little goth barbie girlfriend now. They attacked us," Regina rallied back. "It's time for us to return the favor." Regina opened the door and got into the driver's seat, slamming the door behind her.

Grayson was now definitely yelling and doing so loudly. "Please listen to me, please!" He went to the window, looking for an audience with Regina, while she stared straight forward and cranked the car. He found himself instinctively beating on the glass to get her attention. "This has nothing to do with her or us. I don't want to see you get hurt. These girls are very dangerous."

Veronica, who despite her loyalty to Regina, found her intuition steering her towards trusting Grayson, who was now squatted down by the driver's door nearly in tears, fist resting on the chipped teal paint.

"Grayson, what did you see?" she asked, walking closer to him and catching the corner of Regina's eye.

Grayson stood up, staring right at her. "Whatever. It doesn't matter—she's not going to listen to a word I say. I'm pretty sure they literally broke a girl's arm last night and made her keep playing. Just watch yourselves. Or do whatever the hell you want, but don't say I didn't try and warn you."

He turned away from them and walked back to the door of the roller rink. Orbache and Jerry scattered, from the window where they had been watching the entire meltdown. Veronica walked around to the passenger's side, still looking as Grayson walked away, hoping he would turn around and somehow fix this. But he didn't. Hopes deflated, she opened the door and climbed into the car, concern plastered all over her face.

"What if Grayson is right?" she asked. The foreboding sense of danger fell on deaf ears as the car was slammed into gear and sped out of the parking lot.

Chapter Nine

Dressed for a Funeral

Regina's beat-up, little green Honda barreled down the one-lane service road at the edge of Thimble Woods. She wasn't going anywhere. She was just driving, and driving fast. Veronica's hand had a vice grip on the edge of the stained cloth seat. Out of nowhere and without warning, Regina slammed on the brakes, startling Veronica. She slipped the car into park in the middle of the road and just started crying. She ran her hands over her face—they slid with ease as they glided over her tear moistened cheeks. Veronica didn't know what to say, or what could possibly comfort her. Veronica reached over and turned the key, shutting the car engine off, and removed the key from the ignition. She wasn't sure what to do to help, but right now she knew Regina was in no shape to be behind the wheel.

It was a long time before anything was said. Veronica had stepped out of the car to give Regina some time to herself. Having found an old breadstick in the floorboard of Regina's car, she was now walking along the ditch and feeding stale, crumbling little pieces to the birds. A large black crow watched from a perch above the car. It called out as Regina opened her door and stepped out of the car. She traced a circle in the dust around a spot of hardened pine sap on the hood of her car as she stared into the tree line of the woods.

"I didn't think he would—I didn't know it would bother me this much," Regina finally said. This was probably the first point she had been able to actually stop to think about it. Hurt and heartbreak had been her emotional reaction, and it had been the guttural first response. But now she was beginning to process the information on a cerebral level.

"I broke up with him," she said, as if they both needed a reminder of the order of events. "I shouldn't feel like this," Regina reiterated, trying to rationalize.

She wasn't really sure how she was supposed to feel. Truth be told, she'd never experienced a break-up to this magnitude. Summer flings, dating in high school—she had handled the demise of all of those relationships like a champ. She was never really invested in them. They were nice while they lasted, but she had been none too sad to see them fall apart. But Grayson was different. She was emotionally invested and even that was an understatement. She had regretted breaking up with him the second she had uttered the words, but she was stubborn to a fault. Regina had cut him loose, and he had quickly found his way—his way to someone else. She felt utterly foolish. She chased him away and now was sad that she missed the chance to run after him.

"I know you're not going to believe this," Veronica said, tossing the rest of the breadstick into the woods to the delight of the patient crow who had been playing the long game, "but he's hurting just as bad as you are. Guys are idiots," Veronica reassured. "You broke his heart. And even worse for a guy, you bruised his ego. He jumped into bed with the first thing that made him feel wanted again and offered to turn the sheets down. He still loves you. I know it."

Veronica was sure about that. No matter what or who he had occupied his extracurricular hours, she was sure that he loved her. Veronica had excitedly helped Grayson pick out an engagement ring two years prior, only to have Regina give an impromptu and unfortunately timed speech at dinner one night about how she hated the concept of marriage. Grayson, more than a little defeated, had returned the ring and used the money as part of a down payment when he purchased the roller rink from his uncle to secretly help him cover his medical bills. He had so badly wanted to marry her back then. For two people so much in love, they were often so oblivious to the other.

"No, we're broken," Regina admitted. "This can't be fixed anymore." She was emotionally sobering up and sadly making sense. "I really messed things up." Regina's face scrunched up as she tried to hold back the second round of tears, but it was no use. They poured freely. She wiped her face and turned to Veronica.

"Do you know he wanted to marry me?" Regina asked quietly through the tears. "I never told you, but he had a ring and everything.

I found it in his coat pocket one day. I got scared, and so I did everything I could to try and scare him off from proposing to me without actually just coming out and saying it."

"Oh, Regina," Veronica said with a mix of sadness and disappointment.

"Do you want to know the worst part?" Regina said, followed by what felt like a heavy silence. "I was still really sad that he never actually proposed to me," Regina admitted, crying loudly again. "I wanted to marry that boy so damn much, and he wanted to marry me. Look at me now—I am standing out here in the middle of the woods, dehydrated because I am crying like a child. I just don't understand."

Regina didn't understand. Why did everything have to be so complicated? And now why did everything have to be ruined?

Regina took her sleeve and dried her face.

Her demeanor shifted immediately, back to the true purpose for their leaving the roller rink.

Revenge.

"We should go," she said, holding her hands out for the keys. "We still have a date with the gothic roller girls tonight."

"Are you sure that's a good idea, Regina?" Veronica questioned. "You might not be in the right state of mind for revenge right now."

"Is there a good state of mind for revenge?" Regina asked as she smiled a sad little smile.

Grayson had not taken the time to compose himself before going back into the skating rink. His emotions were still running in overdrive and currently, they were powering a chase around the building as Orbache ran for his safety, continuously apologizing for spilling the beans about Grayson and his night with Bambi. Neither in peak physical shape and both worse for wear, they finally tired, standing a few yards apart panting, out of breath. Grayson grabbed a near empty bottle of cleaner he'd been using to wipe down the tables and threw it at Orbache, nailing him in the head and catching him off guard.

"I said I was sorry," Orbache said, still out of breath. "I swear—it just slipped out."

Grayson stood there with his hands on his knees. He was mad at Orbache, but he was mostly just angry with himself.

"She would've found out eventually," Orbache was telling Grayson something he deep down already knew. "It's not like the two of you were making amends or anything."

He was right on both counts. They were nowhere close to getting back together. And as mad as Grayson was with himself, the simple fact remained that he was single. Aside from some mild southern moral objections to promiscuity, he could sleep with whoever he damn well pleased.

Grayson sat down in one of the booths. His resolve to physically punish Orbache waned as his desire to sit took charge.

"I shouldn't have told them about the practice tonight," Grayson said out of the blue. Not to anyone directly, but just offering the lament to the universe.

Orbache replied, hoping to avoid any further forced exercise while getting back into his friend's good graces, "Yeah, that's going to be one hell of a catfight."

Jerry chimed in, having sat quietly, observing the entirety of the chase and cool down. His slow, heavy southern accent was impressive. It gave him the ability to often sound unaware and uninformed, but then gave these kinds of one-liners power and wisdom. Grayson was grateful for the latter today. "My money's on Regina."

Chapter Ten

Revenge Served Bold

Regina had placed similar odds on herself, as she was once again that week dressed for a funeral, but ready to kick some ass—head to toe in all black in her car, heading to pick up Veronica. She grabbed her phone out of the cup holder and dialed Tabitha's number again. She had been trying to call her all day with no response. The phone went to voicemail again. Regina ended the call and tossed the phone back in the cup holder without leaving a message. She appreciated Tabitha's studious nature, but she really could have used the backup. She pulled up to Veronica's duplex just after sunset and honked the horn once. Code for, "LET'S GO!"

Veronica quickly joined her in the car, holding several bags.

"Is that the stuff?" Regina asked.

Veronica smiled, proud of herself. "Yep! I had to hit up three different craft stores, but I managed to get a ton of the cute bumble bee stickers. They're not going to know what hit them. These bees sting back." She snapped her fingers sassily.

Regina laughed, feeling a little more upbeat. "Yeah, it's hard to be gothic with adorable bumble bee stickers all over everything you own," she laughed again, reinvigorated with the imminent promise of petty vandalism.

Regina slowed down and pulled the car a little too quickly into the thick brush, out of view from the road. The car was parked a block from the hole in the chain-link fence that lined the old warehouse district. Regina shut off the ignition, motioning silently to Veronica. They both stealthily exited the car and started walking along the perimeter, bags in hand as they searched for the gap in the fence.

The hole in the fence was a well known point of access for everyone in the town, as the abandoned warehouses were home to secret parties once or twice every year. No one was ever a hundred percent certain who initiated the festivities, but they never failed to be the biggest blowouts of the year. Grayson's band had played at several of the secret parties over the years, a fact that Regina was trying to ignore as the gnawing feeling of deja vu kept taunting her. She ran her hands along the twisted metal diamonds, still feeling for the break. There was a rhythmic tapping sound as her fingers danced along the wire until she found the hole. In the dark, she motioned for Veronica, and they easily slipped through the large gap in the metal and now found themselves inside the warehouse district.

Their pulses were racing with excitement. Retaliation. Behind one of the smaller free-standing buildings, they could see the faint glow of light. They moved quietly to the top of a small incline and looked down from a better vantage point. They could see the girls. Like a pale emo army on skates, only they weren't skating. They were just standing around, and they all had their gaze affixed on the corner of one of the other warehouses. It was dark, and the shadows hid whatever it was that was going on. Regina couldn't spot Bambi, but from her perch, it was honestly like trying to identify a specific penguin at the South Pole.

"We've got to get closer. I can't see what's going on," Regina whispered. Veronica nodded in agreement.

The two girls scooted down the hill as quietly as possible. For neither of them being very outdoorsy, they managed the descent with surprising skill. Now the only thing between them and the Bloody Mother Suckers was a thin hedge of tall dead grass that flicked back and forth in the breeze followed by twenty yards of loading dock parking. The grass offered minimal coverage, but the pair were well camouflaged thanks to the cloud cover which dulled out the nearly full moon. Their satisfaction with the progress of their plan was painfully short lived. In an instant, the two women were both struck with the sensation that something wasn't right. No, something was very wrong. Neither spoke it, but both felt it deep within their souls. This wasn't just an underground roller derby tournament.

Two bright overhead spotlights flashed on with a loud electric whirr and lit up the previously dark corner of the lot that continued to draw the attention of the Bloody Mother Suckers. There they were, Bambi and her two minions. They were holding something. Regina and Veronica's eyes adjusted to the sudden change.

It was another person. It was a girl—it was two girls. A taller, lanky girl, with her head hanging in front of her. She looked like she had been through hell. And a shorter blonde girl who was clearly crying. Her whimpers travelled in the cool night air.

"Some kind of hazing?" Veronica whispered the question to Regina. It was dumb and juvenile, but even they participated in the ritualistic razzing of new members. The Hunny Bees were guilty of hazing but nothing like this.

Regina was oblivious, not having heard a word Veronica had said. Her eyes were locked on the tall battered girl in the clutches of the enemy. She couldn't take her eyes off her. Something wasn't right, because something about her looked familiar.

Madeline roughly grabbed the short hair of the girl and pulled her head up, illuminating the face of their captive, but Bambi had stepped in front and blocked the view from where Regina and Veronica were crouched.

Bambi began talking, arms outstretched like she was presenting an offering to her followers. "This is it, girls—the spoils of war. Enjoy!"

Bambi then proceeded, in what seemed like slow motion to her audience in the bushes. She opened her mouth and tilted her head back as if she were gasping for air after coming up from the water. She then turned around, and before Regina or Veronica could prepare for what they were about to witness, Bambi turned her head and sank her teeth into the neck of the blonde girl who let out a heart-wrenching scream that fell only on the ears to those present to hear it. Veronica's hand was pressed firmly against her mouth and the other with a vice grip on Regina's arm—it was the only barrier keeping her from screaming and giving away their location. Bambi ripped her head back from the blonde girl's neck, and blood poured from the wounds. She loosened her grip and callously tossed her victim to the ground. The other girls swarmed the fresh kill, quickly sucking it dry of blood, like the weathered nature film of piranhas stripping the flesh from the bone of some unwitting animal.

And then Bambi turned. "And our next prize was chosen by our very own Madeline." She finally stepped out of the way, gesturing to the tall girl whose face was now tragically illuminated from the overhead light.

Regina stood up and screamed out of instinct, forgoing fear and common sense. "TABBY!"

Her face was bruised and hair matted and disheveled, her shirt collar covered in mud and what looked like blood. The girl in the pale hands of Madeline was Tabitha.

The crowd of women turned in Regina's direction in an instant. Like a pack of wild dogs, they raised their heads from the crouched position packed around the body of the small blonde victim. In unison, their gaze narrowed in on her. She couldn't even muster the thought to run, though it would have been pointless even if she would have tried. She and Veronica found themselves standing in the center of a circle of the now very intimidating girls before they were even certain what had happened.

"Let her go," Regina said forcefully, trying her best to shake free of the painful grip two of the derby minions had on her arms. Her protective nature overwhelmed her fear—she stood strong in the face of literal death.

"You just keep showing up uninvited, don't you?" Bambi asked her angrily. Her lips were stained red from the blood of the blonde corpse on the ground just a few feet away, and for the first time up close and in the light, Regina could clearly see two long, pointed teeth resting on her bottom lip.

She had fangs.

"What have you done to her?" Veronica cried. "Tabby, are you okay?" There was no response from Tabitha's slumped body.

"She's fine. For now," Madeline said with a devious smirk. It made her less likeable than she already was.

Tabitha managed to rally enough to force out what sounded like a cry for help from her exhausted and beaten body. The words were faint and nearly unintelligible, but their message landed loud and clear.

"I thought I made it clear I wanted you to stay away from us," Bambi threatened, finding no lightness in the disruption of her evening or the challenging of her authority.

"Fine." Regina seemed strangely agreeable. She was no longer looking for trouble. She'd found more of that than she had bargained for. Now she was bartering to get out of here alive. "Give us Tabitha and we'll go—we will leave you alone. We're gone. We didn't see anything." Regina hoped it would be enough. Truth be told, she had nothing left to offer.

"Regina!" Veronica whispered, shocked that she was overlooking the shriveled up corpse on the ground.

"I don't care," she replied to Veronica. She would let the weight of her selfish will to live plague her with guilt later, but at least they would be alive to do it. Regina turned back and faced Bambi. "Just let her go. We didn't see anything, we don't know anything."

"You killed Greg, didn't you?" Veronica asked.

Regina stared at her, wondering why Veronica insisted on damning them at every step of this escape. Regina was just trying to get them the hell out of this and Veronica suddenly found a backbone.

"I don't even know who that is," Bambi replied mockingly. "But if you mean the wannabe frat boy who reeked of Axe Body Spray and hormones, then yes. We did."

"It was the boy who cried and peed his pants," one of the girls cackled from the crowd.

"Oh my God," Veronica uttered, now more terrified than she knew possible. Her heart ached knowing how the last moments of Greg's life must have been, but now she worried she would share that same fate.

Bambi looked at Regina and raised her eyebrows. "I guess you do know something."

"Kill her," Victoria chanted out from over Bambi's shoulder.

"Please don't," Regina argued for her own preservation. "I don't know what is going on, and I don't care—we just want to go." Her strong tone had begun to falter.

"Oh, please, Regina," Bambi hissed, immune to the pleas of fearful victims. "You're a smart girl. I'm a smart girl. We both know you are working through all of this right now in your brain—you're dancing around it," now imitating her, "'But it can't be, those aren't real,'" she said with a mocking tone.

Bambi leaned forward just a few inches from Regina's face. "But we *are* real."

She opened her mouth and bared her fangs on full display. The two saber-like teeth glistened as they created an indent on her bottom lip, the corners of her mouth turned upward into a smile.

"So, what, you're some kind of roller derby vampire girls?" Regina asked, dumbfounded, and yet she already knew the answer. She was fearing the repercussions even more now and was mentally still trying to figure out how she was going to get them out of this mess.

Bambi erupted in laughter, deep and sinister. It swelled from her core and beckoned the rest of her vampire hyenas to cackle along with her. The laughter was deafening and all-encompassing. Tabitha's head fell back to her chest, not having the strength to muster up the will to continue looking upon her dire surroundings.

"I don't think I have ever heard it put quite like that," Bambi replied, smiling. "I guess we are."

Chapter Eleven

In the Shadow of the Valley of Death

Despite the look of elation on Bambi's face, it did nothing to lighten the mood for her captives. Regina finally comprehended the reality that she was in way over her head. This was not going at all how she had planned. Not that she could have planned for this—how do you plan for this? Her phone was tucked in her back pocket, and she thought she might secretly dial out. A lifeline butt dial. The risk was great and the reward was a slim chance if it reached anyone, and an even more fragile chance that they would believe her.

"What can we do?" Regina asked, not giving up. Not sure what she had to offer. But definitely not ready to die.

"I'm sorry, what?" Bambi looked at her, intrigued. "What *can* you do?"

Regina had nothing to lose at this point. She found her backbone only by last resort—it was this or end up lying in a pool of her own blood like the blonde girl sprawled out mere feet from where she stood.

"What can we do to get Tabby back and for the three of us to leave here alive?" Regina wasn't sure what she was actually offering, but she was sure it was the only chance.

Bambi smiled at her with a look of confusion and a strange tinge of admiration at Regina's will to live. Lots of people had groveled. Many had bargained. But few ever simply asked for a way out. "Let you go? And take her? It's not happening—"

"She's our trophy," Victoria popped her head over Bambi's shoulder and sassily boasted.

Bambi quickly silenced her. "That's enough, Victoria." Victoria slunk back behind her like a scolded pup who had piddled on the floor.

"What kind of trophy?" Regina asked, praying for some leverage in the situation. If nothing else, every minute she kept her talking was another minute she spent among the living.

Bambi paused. It was almost if she was reluctant to respond to her, and for the first time, it appeared Bambi was having to decipher the situation as much as Regina was. It wasn't much, but Regina was clinging to it. One of her wenches had spoken out of turn—it had thrown Bambi off. There was a crack in her pristine presentation of evil. Bambi was afraid that Regina now knew too much. Either swift death or a bargain was next. Regina went double or nothing.

"What kind of trophy?" Regina asked again, more forcefully this time—unsure of where this moxy was coming from but grateful for it nonetheless.

"Derby. A derby prize," Bambi replied. "The ladies and I are competitors in a tournament. Leagues of us all over the country. When you can live forever, entertainment has a way of evolving. We battle it out on the rink. The winner provides the trophy for the next bout." She gave a quick glance to Tabby. "We've won our last eighteen bouts. Your friend here is our next trophy. We play for keeps," Bambi said with intense clarity.

Regina was horrified at the thought of Tabby being bled dry by these women. How long had this been going on? How many Tabithas had there been? Gregs? Blonde girls? Her mind was reeling trying to plan her next move when Veronica made a play of her own.

"We have a team!" Veronica blurted out.

Regina and Bambi seemed equally caught off guard by Veronica's outburst, neither quite certain what to make of it.

"What?" Bambi asked, completely at a loss for words.

In a similar state, Regina also asked point-blank, "Yeah, what?"

Veronica stepped up, only a foot or so away from Bambi. She could smell the metallic residue of blood on her breath. She had a fire in her eyes that Regina had never seen before. Veronica, however, was in fact completely channeling Regina for this bold move. She had stood there silent, realizing she and her best friends were at death's door. Regina was trying to save them, and she had been just standing there frozen in fear. She refused to be afraid anymore. She was living in the valley of the shadow of death, and she was hell-bent on walking out of it.

"The Hunny Bees," she declared. "We have a roller derby team. Let us play you for Tabitha." Veronica was striking a deal.

"Are you out of your mind?" Regina loudly whispered through her teeth, eyes wide. *What the hell was Veronica doing?* she thought to herself.

The comically amused smile that had been resting on Bambi's blood-stained lips faded. She crossed her arms and leaned back, shifting the weight to her back heel. Against her own better judgment, she was considering the offer. For better or worse. "I'm listening," Bambi finally said, absolutely intrigued by the prospect, but by no means fully convinced. Bambi loved nothing more than the sport in the hunt. Veronica's offer had played directly into her morbid desire for blood lust entertainment.

"If we win, then you leave town—immediately." Veronica was writing the conditions as she went. Running blind, guided by hope. "And you never come back. And we get the trophy. We get Tabby. She's ours, like you said, for keeps." Veronica's voice had not faltered, cracked, or wavered. She was a rock. Regina was legitimately impressed, and she could start to feel a shift in power. The negotiating of this proposal was not sitting well with the rest of the girls. They began shifting their weight from side to side, murmuring—some were visibly upset that Bambi was even humoring them, letting fresh blood marinate in conversation, standing right in front of them. Bambi was playing with her food, and some of the team were none too pleased about it.

"And what do we get?" Bambi asked, now much less amused by the whole thing. The conditions definitely felt one-sided.

"I don't know," she suddenly realized. She had nowhere to go. "What do you want?" Veronica had no idea what she was about to have to give up, but every minute spent negotiating was weakening Bambi's resolve. She'd already spent too much time engaging them. Opportunity was on their side.

"Okay, for starters, we keep your friend here. And we wring her out like a sponge while you watch." She paused and smiled. "And I get Grayson." This one was personal. "He'll be my own personal *cock*tail." The strategically placed emphasis reignited a fire in Regina that fear had nearly caused her to extinguish. The arrangement as a whole was sending the team into a chaotic frenzy. Bambi silenced them with a wave of her hand and a quick shush.

"What do you want with Grayson?" Regina asked, furious. "He has nothing to do with this."

Bambi took back the upper hand she knew that she had nearly lost. "I find him fascinating," she said genuinely, but obnoxiously enough to rile Regina up. "Don't worry though, I have no intentions of killing him. Blood isn't the only thing I'm good at sucking—I think he could vouch for that." She was taking pure pleasure in watching Regina squirm. "And I'm pretty sure me being with him would be enough to kill you." She smiled.

"I'm going to kick your ass," Regina said fist clenched, again struggling to force herself free of the flunkies on either side of her.

"Forty-eight hours," Bambi said, ignoring Regina's threat. "You got your wish. Ladies, show our competitors to the fence and see that they don't interrupt us again," Bambi said, turning away from them, now facing Tabitha. She took her hands and lifted her head up again, her black fingernails pressing firmly into her cheeks. She pointed her face towards the girls forcefully escorting Regina and Veronica back towards the fence. "Hear that, sweetheart? Your friends think they can save you." She dropped her hands and let go of Tabitha's face. Her chin hit her chest hard with no resistance. "I wouldn't count on it," Bambi said, walking away. "Put her back in the hole," Bambi barked out at Madeline.

It was in a blur that Regina and Veronica found themselves back at the hole in the fence.

"Don't even think about calling the cops," the dead-eyed, soulless girl said as she pushed them toward the hole in the gate. "We'd kill you and your friends and be gone before they could lie and tell you they'll come to check it out."

"Bambi doesn't make deals," the other girl added. "I certainly hope you don't disappoint her."

Regina and Veronica both crawled through the hole in the fence and found their walk back to the car a silent one, neither speaking. Neither knowing what to say. Regina wasn't sure how long they'd been sitting in the car when she realized she hadn't even put the keys in the ignition—they were resting in her lap, grasped so tightly in her hand that the metal rivets left a blood bruised indention on her palm. Finally, Veronica spoke.

"I know this is probably not the best time to mention this, but I think you owe Jerry an apology." Veronica's face was numb. She wanted to smile. She even thought she might be smiling. But she couldn't help herself from trying to brighten the mood.

Regina looked at her. The times that Veronica had shocked Regina with the words that exited her mouth this evening were becoming impossible to count. "What the hell for?" she asked.

"Well, he was right," Veronica said. "You called him an idiot when he guessed this was all done by vampires."

Regina stared at her, utterly speechless. Then suddenly, she started laughing. She couldn't help but laugh. Veronica joined her. The two, who had been so near to death and the undead just moments before now sat laughing in the car. Laughing in the face of death. The laughter stopped when Regina realized something.

"How am I going to convince the team to play?" Regina said, now realizing this was only the first step in an all uphill battle.

Chapter Twelve
Wish It Were All a Dream

Grayson was torn from a restless sleep by the sound of rattling glass resulting from someone banging intensely on the skating rink door. He immediately and instinctively grabbed the wooden baseball bat that resided between his twin bed and the makeshift bedside table. This wasn't the first time he'd been woken up in the wee hours of the morning by this noise. Drunken college kids often got the idea in the middle of the night that skating would be awesome. The fact the rink was closed rarely phased them. He'd gotten the baseball bat at a yard sale and would brandish it in front of the glass threateningly and the kids would normally run off. Tonight was different. Grayson, still hearing the banging, threw on a pair of pajama pants from the floor, and with the bat in hand, walked out of the small apartment at the rink he'd set up for himself and headed to the door, exhausted and annoyed. He flipped the switch, turning on the small overhead light in the front which also controlled the exterior porch light. There stood Regina and Veronica, clearly distressed, and loudly taking it out on the door. Grayson ran to the door and unlocked it. Before he could even say anything, Regina came in and wrapped her arms around him. Veronica wedged her way in the building around Regina and Grayson and locked the door behind them.

Despite the cool night air still lingering on her sweatshirt pressed up against his bare chest, the embrace was warm. It was familiar and strange at the same time, but it was anything but comfortable. The events of earlier that day still hung heavy in Grayson's mind. Regina buried her head in his shoulder, and when he looked over at Veronica, it was glaringly obvious she'd been crying. Grayson put his hands on Regina's arms and gently pried her off of him.

"Do you guys have any idea what time it is?" he asked. He tried to sound more annoyed than he was. He was more concerned than anything.

"They've taken Tabby!" Regina almost yelled, tears welling up in her eyes.

"Who has taken Tabitha? What do you mean?" Grayson asked, still not one hundred percent awake. He was struggling to keep up with what was happening, and uncertain it wasn't all a dream. "What's going on?"

"We went to their practice tonight," Veronica told him as if she was confessing something, holding her head down.

Grayson started pacing out of frustration that they had done the one thing he had asked them not to do. "What did I tell you guys?! I told you those girls are—"

"They're vampires, Grayson. They're vampires," Regina interrupted. She knew the words sounded stupid. She knew she sounded crazy, and maybe she was. But she was right. "They took Tabby, and they are going to drain her if we can't beat them in a derby bout!" she finished, spilling it all out to a blank-faced and confused Grayson.

"Vampires?" he asked, as any sane person would, with laughable doubt.

"They killed Greg," Veronica said, wiping her face. "And some blonde girl, right in front of us." She began to cry. "Bambi just, her fangs—she, she bit her, and they drank from her like a piece of fruit."

Grayson looked at the two of them. There he stood in the middle of a dimly lit vestibule, shirtless, holding a baseball bat, and surrounded by two women in tears talking about vampires. He was overwhelmed. If it was a dream, it was turning into a nightmare.

"I think I need to sit down," he said.

"There's no time for sitting!" Regina urged. "I have to get the derby team together, we have to battle them to save Tabby in two days! If we don't win, they are going to kill her, and she's going—" Her eyes met his, those sleepy, grey, kind eyes hanging on her every ridiculous word. She quickly looked away, hoping he hadn't noticed the pause. "I have to get the girls together. We have to practice."

Grayson had definitely noticed the uneasy pause. "What aren't you telling me, Regina?" There was a firmness in his voice. It wasn't cruel, and as he repeated the question following silence, it was much less understanding than he had been moments before. "Regina, what are you not telling me?"

Regina turned away from him. Her hands up at her face, she struggled not to hyperventilate.

"You were part of the bargain, too," Veronica answered for her.

He looked back over at Regina—fear now plagued those grey eyes. "They're going to kill me?" he asked. "Look at me, Regina," he begged, but she refused or was unable—either way, she remained stoic. "They're going to kill me? You used me as leverage?"

"No. She did," Regina said, finally turning to him. He had to know it wasn't her. She hadn't purposefully made him part of any of this. "They're not going to kill you. She was pretty clear about it," Regina clarified. It was good news that he wasn't to be killed, but there was a heavy sadness in her tone.

Grayson stood there for quite some time, silently trying to process everything. Trying to come to terms with the reality that he was now the pawn in a battle of literal life and death. When he finally decided to speak, it wasn't what either had expected to hear. Regina had honestly half expected him to throw them out. But he hadn't.

"You know they're really good," he calmly said.

And she did—Regina knew this was not going to be easy. "I know," she said, "but we don't have a choice."

Grayson ran his hands through his hair and scratched his head as if he was trying to force his brain into action. "Okay. I'll go grab some blankets. I might have another pillow. You guys should stay here tonight. You've got to get some rest. You are no good exhausted—"

"Grayson, we have to do something! Now!" Veronica nearly exploded, feeling Grayson was missing the urgency of the situation. "Tabby is still there!"

He continued, undeterred. "We'll sleep until sunrise. Then you," pointing at Regina, "you get on the phone and get all the girls here as quickly as you can. We have to use daylight to our advantage. If they are vampires, they'll rest while the sun is out. I hope." Grayson was basing much of his plan on knowledge gathered from cartoons and Abbott and Costello movies, but that was the only point of research he had at this point. "That's when we need to be working as hard as we can. I'll close the rink. You can have the entire day to practice. But for now, you need to sleep. Neither of you is going to be worth shit if you don't get some sleep."

The girls couldn't argue. Grayson had finally taken charge when it was most important. Somehow in spite of all of this, he was calm and collected. He was thinking straight because he knew he had to—the girls couldn't right now. They needed a rock. Regina had been that for him before, and he would not miss the opportunity to repay her for that. He was proof at this point that people can surprise you. For as half-assed as he seemed to live his life, he was wholeheartedly heroic in their hour of need.

They made a pallet of blankets on top of the thin foam mats Grayson used to help younger kids first learning to skate on the floor of his apartment. He locked the door and moved a dresser up against it. It was a depressing slumber party to say the least. The floor was hard and the thin mats and blankets did little to remedy that. Veronica laid on the floor staring up at the ceiling tiles, silent tears running down her face. She was struggling to find sleep. Sleep required her to close her eyes, and every time her eyes shut, all she could see was the blonde girl laying on the asphalt, blood staining her hair and clotting in the little gold chain that hung around her neck. Her eyes still open, still crying for help even in the afterlife. That girl probably had a family. She had friends who would miss her. Maybe even a cat or a tiny dog. It had been expecting her home tonight. For some reason, the thought of this tore her up inside even more. The thought of a little dog waiting at the door with love and loyalty to a master that it would never see again. Her breath caught in her throat as she struggled to breathe through the tears.

"You have to stop crying," Grayson's voice broke through the dark room. It was stern and comforting at the same time. "Please get some sleep. We'll get her back," he reassured. "I promise we're going to figure this out." His words were soothing. The girls who had spent all evening trying to be strong, facing the world here and after by themselves, were finally able to let someone else be strong for them. At least until morning.

Grayson was lying. He had no idea how any of this was going to work out, but he knew one thing: crying wasn't going to solve it. Neither would panicking. He would have to do his best to try and stay level headed for all three of them. It was actually advantageous to have something to concentrate on. It saved his mind wondering what would become of him if the girls couldn't prevent this all from happening.

Chapter Thirteen

In This Together

Sunrise came quietly under the haze of a foggy, damp November morning. The alarm Grayson had set on his phone chimed for nearly fourteen minutes before it finally ripped him away from a deep, dream-filled sleep. He hit the snooze in the event he dozed back off and laid there motionless in his bed, eyes open and letting his dreams fade from memory. As the last fragments of a confusing, frightening fantasy slipped from his consciousness, he was brought back to reality. He was living in a nightmare—the last thing he needed was to let the ones linger around from his sleep. He crawled out of the bed and silently stepped over the girls, who still slept on the floor. He pushed the dresser away from the door and walked out to the rink.

It was still dark, but a little sunlight bled into the rink from the windows in the vestibule. The few streaks of light that crept in were speckled with dust dancing in the air. He rarely looked at it like this. He rarely looked around like it might be his last opportunity to do so. The rink was old—it wasn't much to look at, but it was his. Grayson wondered what would become of the rink if he were to be taken by Bambi. He wasn't really sure what it meant for him, but he was fairly sure he wouldn't be able to stay here. He walked over and started a pot of coffee with the small coffee maker in the little office near the front counter. He sat down at the computer, bathed in the blue light from the glowing screen in the dark room. He clicked the icon to get him to the Internet and typed the word "vampires" into the search engine. The screen lit up with *Twilight*, *True Blood*, even an interview with the band "Vampire Weekend" popped up. He amended his search, adding the word "real." The new search results now brought up articles about real-life "vampire" teens cutting into their skin and sucking on each others' blood. It was a lot of disturbed people and drug-fueled delusions. He scrolled down until he saw a blurb about an unsolved crime in New Hampshire on a blog.

Roberta Drake, 54, of Haverhill, stated that she had come upon the scene and witnessed several girls attacking the victim. They were crouched over the body of Rita York, 34, a local mother. Furthermore, it was reported that when the attackers heard Drake approaching, they stood up and seemed to glide away. Drake unsuccessfully attempted to aid the victim. York was pronounced dead at the scene. Authorities are looking for anyone with details on the unusual crime, which left the victim nearly completely devoid of bodily fluids, particularly blood. An ongoing investigation continues.

Grayson was fairly certain he was on the right track. He typed in the name of the victim and found her obituary. Rita York had been a mother. She had two small children, and she had also been the coach of a roller derby team. Grayson was now convinced this was not a coincidence. He was sure that she was another victim of the Bloody Mother Suckers. *Their name makes a lot more sense now,* he thought to himself. How better to hide than in plain sight? He continued reading, looking for related links or stories. He was staring at the screen so intently, it startled him when Regina appeared in the doorway.

At some point during the night, she must have changed into one of Grayson's shirts. She looked radiant in the cool light of the monitor. Grayson looked at her like he'd looked at her so many times before. His eyes followed from her face down past one of his band's old concert merch tees to her bare legs. He quickly turned his eyes back to the screen, guilty—those legs were no longer his to see.

"Your phone was still going off," she said. "Why didn't you wake us up?" It was the first time in days they had spoken to each other when it wasn't insults or life and death. She missed it.

"I just hit the snooze. I thought you guys could use the extra nine minutes," he replied, smiling and offering a little nod in her direction.

Regina sat down on a short filing cabinet next to the door. "I was worried," she said. "I woke up and didn't see you there. I was afraid that she'd . . . I was afraid you were gone," Regina admitted. There was no pretense or motive behind it. In that brief moment, the walls were down.

"I'm not going anywhere. We're in this together," he reached over and put his hand on top of hers, which was resting on her knee. "Okay?"

"Okay," she replied, giving the slightest hint of a sad smile.

His hand lingered there for a moment. He hadn't even thought about the response, but he began to feel the warmth of her skin beneath his and quickly drew it back, leaning back in the desk chair. "You should probably start calling the girls," he said. "What are you even going to tell them?" he said with a laugh.

Regina sat quiet and bit her bottom lip. "I don't know. I just need to get them all here, and then I'll figure something out."

Grayson grabbed a yellow legal pad that was sitting on the desk, took a black permanent marker, and wrote in large letters on the page.

RINK CLOSED
MAINTENANCE

"Before I forget," Grayson said as he stood up to go tape the sign to the door. "When that's ready, would you pour me a cup?" he asked her, pointing at the coffee machine.

She nodded. "How do you like it?" The seemingly normal question slipped out of her mouth.

He smiled. It was the first time she'd seen him smile like that in a long time. "Black," he said. And gave a quick wink and walked out the door.

That had always been their little joke—she had asked out of habit, muscle memory. Regina knew how he liked his coffee. He actually took it with a little milk, but the first time they had ever gone out on a date, it had gone well. So well, that they had gone to grab a coffee the next morning. When the waitress had asked him how he liked his coffee while ordering, Grayson, as cheesy as ever, responded, "Black, like I like my women." And he had given Regina that same wink that she had just seen again. It was cringeworthy, and had she not been so into him, it would have been enough to send her packing. But she was, and if she wasn't sure before that moment, she knew then. This was no ordinary guy. Their crabfaced waitress hadn't found it as endearing. She rolled her eyes and walked away.

Regina sat on the filing cabinet and watched him walk away. With the circumstances as they were, with the vampires and threat of death, they had been too preoccupied to focus on how much they hated each other or hated that they still loved each other. Right now, things were in such a weird place. She was so lost in thought that when Veronica came and put her hand on her shoulder, it scared her to the point where she screamed loudly. Grayson came running back into the room.

Out of breath, he asked, "What? What happened?"

"I scared her," Veronica said.

"Why in the fuck would you do that?" Grayson asked, astounded at Veronica's stupidity.

"I wasn't *trying* to scare her!" she replied, a bit annoyed with Grayson for thinking she had purposefully scared Regina.

"Sorry, she startled me. Everything is fine," Regina said, trying to calm Grayson down. It was sweet to see him so protective of her. She tried to shake the thought from her head.

Veronica grabbed the coffee pot and poured her a mug. "I think we're all just a little jumpy," she said, walking over and turning on the TV. She flipped the channel over to the local morning news. The weather was partly cloudy. They'd missed the five-day breakdown. *Not that it matters,* she thought. They might be dead by then anyway. The meteorologist sent it back over to the news desk, and the chipper female anchor did a quick tone shift and introduced the next news clip. A little house with grey siding and hunter green shutters popped up on the little 17-inch TV screen. A reporter stood in front of yellow police tape. Grayson realized he recognized the house.

"Turn it up!" he yelled. "Turn the volume up!" he repeated with barely a breath in between.

Veronica cranked the volume up, confused.

The news reporter told the story of how the neighbors had been concerned when the Hearthsides had not been seen or heard from in several weeks. Thanks to a wellness visit, the police had made the gruesome discovery. Dale and Linda Hearthside, the sweet older couple on Cherry Street, were found dead in the box freezer in their basement, immaculately preserved. The sheriff referred to it as skilled amateur embalming. The reporter shot it back to the news desk, and there was a commercial break. Regina and Veronica turned and looked at Grayson. The color had left his skin—it was as if he'd seen a ghost.

"I was in that house," he uttered, barely opening his mouth to speak. "I was in their bedroom. I was in their bed," he divulged. "And they were dead in the basement." Grayson was realizing his involvement in all of this was more wrapped up and tangled and demented than he knew.

Shocked at this new revelation, Veronica asked, "When?"

Grayson looked over at Regina. "The night she took me home," he said, so ashamed of himself, and hating that he ever had to repeat any of these details in front of Regina. "She took me to that house. She said that they were staying with friends. I remember leaving the house the next morning."

"Grayson, you had no way of knowing," Veronica said, seeing that he was clearly upset. "You can't blame yourself for that. None of us knew any of this was going on."

Her words offered little comfort. To him or Regina.

"I've got some calls to make." Regina stood up and left the room. The comfort of forgetting the break-up had ended. Regina was now reminded that he had been with her, in that house. In their bed.

Chapter Fourteen
The New Recruits

It was before eight in the morning, Regina had managed to either get a hold of all the girls or leave messages asking them to meet her at the rink at ten. She could only pray they would come, a silent prayer she whispered under her breath. She refused to allow herself to think about the other side of the coin if her team refused to show up, or even worse, refused to play.

She had gotten her skates out of the trunk of her car and was making circles around the rink—for no other reason than to clear her head. Veronica had dozed off in a booth, having not slept well, while Grayson remained sequestered in the office on the computer, looking for any shred of information on the reality of vampires, and avoiding awkward eye contact with Regina.

As tragic as it was enlightening, Grayson had discovered nearly thirty separate reported deaths that fit the modus operandi of the derby girls. Several of them were hundreds of miles away on the same day. Grayson believed that he had found the work of at least two of the other teams that played in the secret league of the undead—one of which he speculated to be native to Northern California, or possibly Seattle. And the thing that he had begun to put full faith in was that the vampires were not easy to stop. In fact, from what he could tell, they had never been stopped. This began to gnaw away at Grayson. Every fiber was stricken with the nagging question of why they would have let the girls go last night. He was missing something, something he feared was critical.

With this sinking feeling in his soul, he got up, briefly leaving his post. He went to the storeroom and removed a wooden broom from the corner, gripping it with his hands about shoulder width apart. At full force he rammed it into the door frame, snapping the broom handle into two pieces. He held a foot-long shard of wood in his hand, letting the rest of the broom fall to the floor as he went back to the office. He clenched his hands when he sat back down. The snapping of the wood had reverberated more than he had expected and his hands still tingled, but he forged ahead. Grayson dug around and took out an old pocket knife from the desk drawer. He silently shut the door with his foot and began shaving down the wood with the knife. Flecks of broom handle dropped into the trashcan as he whittled away.

As Regina went around the rink, she did everything she could to not think about the flirtation between her and Grayson that morning. Even if she was ready to forgive him, and he forgave her, and they reconciled...she wouldn't. She couldn't bear to even consider it. She refused to let herself fall back into him and then have him taken from her again. She couldn't let herself lose him again. Regina was deep in thought when Orbache walked past her into the office with Grayson.

"So, what the hell is so damn important that you couldn't tell me over the phone?" he wailed at Grayson as he swung open the office door. Orbache always seemed to be in a hurry for no reason, no matter what the circumstance was. It was a product of his upbringing—never waiting for anything didn't make him a patient man. It was rare that he didn't get what he wanted right when he wanted it. He was always being dragged away for something less important or interesting than what he was having to leave. Grayson always saw it as one of the downsides to having money. Wealthy people, to Grayson, always seemed to possess a certain unjustified self-importance. Orbache was sadly no exception.

Grayson motioned for him to shut the door, and Orbache took a seat on the small ratty armchair that was resting against the far wall. "Seriously, dude—why so hush-hush?" he asked as he kicked off his shoes, making himself at home.

Grayson set the knife and the remnants of the broom handle on the desk, which was now taking on a dagger-like shape, leaning forward with a squeak of the chair. He faced Orbache, who still seemed to lack a grasp of the seriousness of the situation. "Okay, look. I need to tell you something, and I need you to just trust me. Don't ask questions—just trust what I'm about to tell you." Grayson wasn't sure how to preface this any other way.

"Is Regina pregnant?" Orbache's eyes went wide and he jumped up in the chair, crouched like a giddy gargoyle—finally comprehending that this was serious, just so, *so* very far off base. "Is she?"

Grayson shook his head, honestly not having expected that, but realizing he should've. "No. She's not pregnant. Just give me a second, okay?" He paused. "There is, um—" Grayson was struggling to get any of this out. "Okay, look—Regina and Veronica have gotten mixed up in an underground roller derby league that happens to be comprised of vampires. Swear to God. Real-life, blood-sucking, dangerous vampires. And Bambi is their leader."

Orbache slid back into the seat and sat quietly for a moment, letting it all sink in—processing every detail of what had just been revealed to him. Grayson waited, unsure if Orbache would believe him. In all honesty, why would he? It was all quite unbelievable. Finally, an inquisitive look came across Orbache's face. "Did you have sex with a vampire?"

"Is that really what you got out of all of that?" Grayson asked, slightly annoyed that he wasn't at least a little surprised or concerned. "Yes—I guess the answer is yes."

"She didn't bite you, did she?" Orbache asked, this time with a noticeable reverence for the predicament, pulling the collar of his jacket closed slightly.

"No," Grayson responded.

"Good. You know that's how they turn you," he said. "If they bite you and don't drain you, you become one of them. It's how they recruit new members." Orbache leaned back into the chair. His phrasing clicked immediately with Grayson, who stared straight at him.

"That's it," Grayson nearly shouted, pointing at Orbache. "That's why! That's why they agreed to battle them," Grayson realized, thinking out loud. "They are going to recruit them." Grayson jumped up from the chair and grabbed the broom handle off the table. He swung open the door and stormed out of the room.

A look of pure fear and confusion washed across Orbache's face. "Wait! Were you being serious?" he called out, nearly an octave higher than his normal register. "They're real vampires!?" he asked, jumping up and following Grayson out the door, nearly tripping on his own shoes on the floor that he had so casually kicked off just moments before.

Regina was still making circles around the rink when Grayson walked out into the middle, waving his hands and calling out for her to stop. She whipped around, pulling up to a stop in front of him.

"You find something?" Regina asked, hoping for something—anything at this point.

"They're trying to recruit you! All the girls. They don't want to give you the chance to win back Tabitha. They are looking to round out their team roster," Grayson said with the conviction of a man who had seen the light.

"No, that's—no, they are playing us." Regina was refusing to see it. She argued with him, "She said she would give us the chance to win her back. It's all about the competition to them."

"Here, I made you something." Grayson took the sharpened broom handle and handed it to her. He had whittled it to a surprisingly sharp point.

"It's a sharp stick," Regina replied, not intending to sound ungrateful.

"It's a stake." Grayson said. "This is how you're going to have to kill her."

"Kill her?" Regina was caught off guard. "I have no plans of killing anyone. All we have to do is win the bout, and they'll let us go!" Regina exclaimed. "I don't have to kill her." She refused to believe that this was no longer a winnable scenario.

"Regina—win or lose, they're not going to let any of us out of there alive," Grayson told her plainly.

"He's right," Veronica said, walking up from behind him, having been stirred from her nap by the commotion. Veronica agreed with him. "They're never going to let us go. It's either us or them."

"But why me? Why do I have to kill her?" Regina asked, almost pleading not to have to do the deed. Regina wasn't a killer. She wasn't like them.

"You'll have the best access to her," Grayson replied. "Baby, it's gotta be you."

She nodded, realizing she didn't have a choice. As a jammer, she would be pitted head-to-head with Bambi. "Okay, I can do it," she said, still a lingering reluctance in her voice. She took the homemade stake in her hand and gripped it with purpose. She looked at it in her hand, trembling with adrenaline and fear, she stuck it in between her jeans and her belt. "How am I supposed to kill them all though?" she asked.

"I don't think you have to," Grayson responded. "I found something online. Do you remember the first time you met her at their practice?"

Regina slightly angered, remembering the encounter more for her and Grayson's interaction answered, "Vividly. There had better be a point to this trip down memory lane."

"There is," Grayson said. "They hung on her every word, almost like she controlled them. And you told me last night that she almost commanded the team to be quiet. I think they are blood bound."

Veronica concurred, "Yeah, she just waved her hand and it silenced them."

Orbache chimed in, "What is blood bound?" Orabache's head was spinning. He was trying to take everything in and catch up—his eyes dashed back and forth from each of them as they spoke.

"She's the matriarch of the coven," Grayson explained. "Either she has been responsible for creating the vampires on her team or she keeps them by feeding them. As long as she is the one who always bites the victims first, then she'll let the team feed, and it forms a psychological bond. As long as they are fed, it makes it nearly impossible for them to disobey her. They have come to depend on her for food, to stay alive. It's caused them to go into a trance called blood bound. If you kill her, the rest should scatter like roaches when the lights are flicked on. I think it breaks the bond somehow."

"Are you sure?" Regina asked. It sounded too good to be true.

"Honestly? No," Grayson answered, a little thrown off by the expectation of real information. "We're talking about vampires here, Regina." He paused, realizing how defensive he was coming off and back peddled into a softer mode. "There isn't like real actual science out there on the subject. There is this guy who is a professor out west—he has a blog where he writes these pseudo-academic hypotheses about vampires and other supernatural creatures, but mostly about vampires." He tried to impress upon her his gut feeling about it. "It reads like he has done real research—pages and pages of it." Grayson shrugged. "It's the best we've got."

"Good to know," Regina said, simply appreciative that Grayson hadn't even questioned her once about what she and Veronica had seen the night before. He had just believed her.

Orbache, still slightly freaking out, asked, "So, this is really real?"

Chapter Fifteen

When We All Arrive

Not long after their conversation, the team began showing up. Many of them were none too pleased about this last-minute meeting. The girls were sitting in the concession area occupying the booths, but Regina was nowhere to be found. Getting a group of derby girls together and then making them wait was not the wisest of moves. As they began to get restless, Grayson and Veronica both sensed that the group's morale was fading fast. He needed to go get Regina.

"Stall them!" Grayson told Veronica. He ran in the back to find Regina. "She can't have gone far. I'll find her."

Sure enough, she had not gone far. She was sitting in Grayson's apartment on his bed, legs crossed. Grayson grabbed a folding wooden chair, slid it up next to the bed, and sat down.

"The girls are all here," he said gently. "Everyone showed up but Lizzy. They're waiting on you out there."

She turned, looked him right in the eyes, and shook her head. "I can't do this," she admitted. "I can't do this. I can't lead them. Grayson, I'm scared." She was fighting back tears as she wobbled slightly back and forth.

"Good, it's good to be scared," Grayson said, reaching up and putting both his hands on her knees, reassuring her.

She looked at him, confused.

"You're going to need that fear. You're going to feed off that fear," he told her, leaning down a little to meet her eyes. "Like you did the first day I met you. You were afraid to get out there on those skates—you were nervous to even come to the rink." He smiled. "I remember that girl, Regina. Her knees were bouncing, her palms were sweaty, and she was wearing cartoon cat socks. But you did that, and you can do this. I know you can."

"What if I can't?" Her shoulders raised slightly then sharply dropped. Regina doubted herself now more than ever. "Grayson, if I can't do this people die. Real people, and it will be my fault. Tabitha will die if I don't win."

"You will. Cause you're not going to let anything happen to her or me," Grayson really did believe that. "It's not in your nature to let the people you care about to get hurt." Grayson told her. "You won't let it happen."

"But I hurt you. I care about you, and I let you get hurt," Regina said. "So you're kind of full of shit. Your theory doesn't work."

"Regina, we're both at fault," he said, maybe the first time ever really owning up to his mistakes in their relationship. "I slept with someone else. I think we're even." He had sincerely not meant any malice by the statement nor had intended to anger her. He honestly just wanted to put everything behind them—forget all of the hate and just move on. But when he said it, he had seen a flicker, a fire in her eye. It gave him a foolishly dangerous idea. It was either genius, or he would go down in flames. He took a chance and poked the bear. "Of course, we were broken up."

"For a week, Grayson," she replied, although her annoyance was barely noticeable. "Let's just drop it."

"You're right. It didn't mean anything. We were broken up. No harm done, right?" he said, walking a tightrope.

"No harm done?" Regina raised her voice slightly and cocked her head to the side. "You slept with someone else! I'm not just going to forget that."

"Well, me neither—if you know what I mean," Grayson half-joked.

"Are you kidding me right now?!" Regina asked, now sitting up on her knees, arms crossed. "We were broken up for seriously like ten minutes, and you jumped into the bed of the first girl who looked at you! Do you really expect me to be okay with that?" She was finally getting really angry.

"She did more than look at me," Grayson said, raising his eyebrows provocatively.

"I know you are not going to seriously sit here and start telling me about the two of you having sex," Regina said her eyes were wide. She was livid.

Grayson was about to take it a step further.

"No, no, no—don't think of it like that. Sorry, I don't want you to ever compare yourself to her, you're both . . . good. She was just different, so uninhibited. She said you were probably just a little uptight, it wasn't your fault. What did she call you . . . 'Repressed Regina.'" Grayson had taken it to the limit—even he wasn't sure if he had taken it too far. He braced for impact.

Regina jumped up off the bed. "I'm about to kill that bitch," Regina erupted. "I'll show that pale, boney, bloodsucker repressed!" Grayson stood up with a slight smile and followed her to the door. Before she left the room, she turned around and kissed him on the cheek. "Thanks, I needed that."

"You focus better when you're distracted and angry. Thankfully, I know a thing or two about getting you there," he said, smiling.

She left the doorway, then quickly turned back to Grayson. "Just out of curiosity, how much of that was true?" she asked.

"Regina, I was drunk. I don't really remember much of anything," he admitted.

She looked at him.

"Except she had the most perfect breasts," he added.

"Too far."

Her face went into a scowl, and she whipped around and went heading towards the rink. Grayson smiled again.

Chapter Sixteen
Sending A Message

Regina marched out to the rink and climbed up onto one of the tables. The fluorescent light behind her gave her a glowing presence. Her stance was powerful, and when she spoke, it was commanding. If Grayson had squinted, she might have passed for a superhero.

"Ladies, one of our own has been taken," Regina started. "I called you all here today because we are all in danger." The girls all looked at each other in disbelief and confusion. Regina continued, "The Bloody Mother Suckers are a team of roller derby vampires, and they have kidnapped Tabitha and plan on draining her unless we can beat them in an underground derby bout." There was an exchanging of glances that peppered the awkward silence. The team stared at Regina, who had seemingly finished some kind of strange, brief motivational speech, a mix of strained confidence and raw emotion, mixed with absolute insanity.

At that point, the girls were done. Regina had dragged them from their day to come and listen to what could only be a drunken rant fueled by a rough break-up. Several of them stood up and began angrily walking to the door. Regina attempted to stop them. "They're going to kill her!" Regina said frantically, trying to salvage everything. "I understand what I just said sounds absolutely crazy, but it's not.

It's real and we are really in this—this is happening. I saw them kill a girl last night with my own eyes." Regina was practically screaming. But the girls were still heading for the door.

In their way, however, was Elizabeth Ackerage—better known as Lizzy Borden, a newer member of the team. Her blonde hair was disheveled, her eyes bloodshot, puffy, and red, having been rubbed raw. She white-knuckled a small chain in her left fist. She was late to the meeting but must have been standing in the foyer since the beginning of Regina's speech. She looked like she had been through hell. "Listen to her. She's telling the truth," Lizzy uttered, the remark stung with pain and a disconnect from the world around her. "Slayer is telling the truth."

"And why should we believe you?" Mindy Mayham crossed her arms and asked her, ill-mannered, wanting nothing more than to get back to her "Grey's Anatomy" marathon she had planned for herself this weekend.

"Because Regina saw them kill my sister," she said vacantly. Her grasp loosened, and the small star charm slipped from her hand and dangled in the open space between the floor and her fist.

Veronica saw the glimmer of the star and immediately recognized the little celestial shape that had haunted her dream. Her hands went to her face and tears ran down her cheeks. The blonde girl had been Lizzy's sister.

"She went out with some friends two nights ago and never came home," Lizzy told them. "They found her this morning like she had been mummified, just dried up . . . with puncture wounds on her neck." She stared into nothing, and for a few moments, the room was silent. Mayham's arms uncrossed, and she shifted uncomfortably in her own skin. And then suddenly, there was a collective consciousness amongst the team. Regina was telling the truth.

Regina broke the silence. Her tone lacked the same call to action as before—she was now more matter of fact. "I'm gonna need every single one of you," she said, trying to rally. "You girls are the best out there, and if I don't have you, there is no way we can win. And we have to win, or more people are going to die. People we know. And people we care about." She looked over at Grayson, who was propped up against the counter. "Please, I need your help. I can't do this without you. I won't do this without you. You're my team."

There was another long silence. The team's eyes bore holes in the floor as each member stared downward, waiting for someone else to speak.

"You don't touch one of our own," a firm voice finally called out. "You hurt one of us, you hurt all of us." Esther, a middle-aged, busty redhead, also known as Bloody Mary, stood up, putting her arm around Lizzy. "We'll help you, Regina. You're our captain. We trust you."

One by one, the other girls stood up. It nearly moved Regina to tears. In her time of need, these girls had come through for her. They were her team, her family. Regina wasn't giving herself enough credit, however. They were coming through for her, but they had a strong leader. Regina was about to lead a team into the unknown. What she was attempting was impossible, but accomplishments are only inhibited by reality, so Regina chose to ignore the fact that they indeed might fail.

"Well, are we going to stand around here, or are we going to practice?" Veronica shouted, her voice cracking, as she wiped tears from her face. "They're good—we've seen them play. They play dirty, and they don't mind hurting us or one another. We're going to need all the practice we can get. Regina is in jammer position, and the goal in the bout is to make sure she can get to their jammer. She's their leader."

"I don't want to just beat them, Regina," Lizzy said through gritted teeth. "I want to kill them. I want to kill them all." Tears ran down her face as she spoke. Bloody Mary hugged her tightly, but she rejected the embrace. She shook her head, swallowed hard, and stood tall. "I'm ready to skate."

The girls all quickly laced up. There was surprisingly little chatter amongst the team as they readied to go out on the rink. Lizzy caught up to Regina as they were about to begin.

"Can I talk to you?" Lizzy asked quietly. Regina didn't know her very well—she was one of the quieter girls on the team. She was always dressed like she came straight from work to practice. Frazzled, but trying to maintain some professionalism. Regina typically thought she looked like a bank teller. But she was fragile and raw now.

"Lizzy, I am so sorry. I didn't know she was your sister. Why did you even come to this meeting? You should be with your family," Regina said, not knowing what to say, but knowing that if anyone got a free pass for this, it was Lizzy.

"I should," Lizzy quietly agreed, but there was a disconnect. "I know I probably shouldn't be here, but I can't help it. Regina, I have a daughter—" Lizzy began to say, but was quickly cut off by Regina.

"I know. Go, I understand. You don't have to do this," Regina told her, trying to be an understanding coach and woman.

"No, you don't understand," Lizzy retaliated, softly frustrated that Regina wouldn't let her get out the full thought. "I have a daughter. I don't want her growing up in a world where vampires aren't just on

God awful TV shows or cheap costumes at a Halloween store." Regina exhaled the slightest hint of a laugh, but there was no humor to be found. "I want to do everything I can to stop them. And I came here because I knew you were going to be the only one who would believe me when I told you. Regina, I came because they were sending you a message."

"What do you mean?" Regina asked, horrified. Her hairs stood on end.

"My sister was wearing an Upstate Nowhere shirt." Lizzy stared at Regina, knowing she knew what that meant.

And indeed, the words struck Regina like a freight train. Her heart sank into her stomach. She knew those words—she knew exactly what they meant. Upstate Nowhere was Grayson's band. She herself had dozens of the local indie rock bands' shirts. She had worked the merch table at too many concerts to count. Her breath came out shallow. She held it as she prepared herself to hear the next words. Her message from the undead.

"The one with the album cover, with the guys' pictures." Lizzy described a shirt Regina was intimately familiar with. "Regina, Grayson's was gone. His picture was the only one torn out of the shirt. I don't think that was a coincidence."

"It's not. She wants him." Regina turned and looked over at Grayson, who was talking to Orbache. "And I will die before I let that happen," Regina said, resolute.

"Regina, that's probably the idea," Lizzy said somberly as she turned away from her and hopped out on the rink.

Chapter Seventeen

Last Chances and Poor Choices

The ominously prophetic comment evaporated from Regina's skin like sweat as she stepped out onto the floor. She donned the black cloth cap with the large gold star and the little felt bumblebee, sliding it carefully over her helmet. She took a deep breath. She had done these runs hundreds of times before, but today was different. *Everything is different,* she thought to herself. It was time to push those thoughts to the deepest part of her consciousness and go out there and just skate. Lead the team and win. Winning was her only option. Her hand grazed the wooden dagger that was tucked in her belt, concealed by a small makeshift sheath she'd made from a pocket she'd ripped out of her duffle bag. A hard reminder of the literal and figurative stakes of this game. No matter the outcome of this bout, someone was going to end up dead.

The team began by running several warm-up drills. Weaving in and out in tandem lines, duck walking, suicides—Regina masterfully checked off the drills. She was doing her best to conduct this as normally as any other practice. The team clung to her every command, and for a moment, she briefly felt the power that she imagined Bambi lorded over her team. But Regina was better. Regina had earned it fair and square. Hard work. She didn't use tricks and mysticism—she commanded true respect.

Grayson and Orbache had begun to set up a makeshift assembly line in the back, making sandwiches for the girls. Orbache had left the rink earlier and gone to the store against Grayson's better judgment. Grayson wasn't sure how, but he was certain if there was any way possible, the vampires would have the rink under surveillance, watching the comings and goings to get the upper hand on Regina.

"They don't know me," Orbache has argued. "They have no reason to worry about me. Plus, the sun is still out," he had told Grayson as he left, trying to ease what Orbache thought was unneeded caution. Orbache didn't like feeling trapped. He spent hours upon hours in that rink, but today it felt claustrophobic. He needed the mental break and the fresh air.

He had returned without incident, as expected, bearing several loaves of bread and a random assortment of sandwich fixings along with a number more obscure additional items Grayson had secretly scribbled on the back of a gas receipt while Regina was otherwise occupied on the floor. He took the bags and tucked them behind the chair in the office, not mentioning another word of it, even to Orbache. No clarification. He simply took it from him and hid the items.

Orbache had understood the practicality of most of the seemingly unconnected items. A couple of flashlights, batteries, glow sticks, and half a dozen bottles of caffeine pills were mostly obvious to Orbache as to why they had made Grayson's covert list. There were several items he couldn't quite figure out, though, and he hoped he would soon be made privy to the plan. Razor blades, lighters, kerosene, electrical tape, boxes of matches, spray bottles, spray paint—they were the items Orbache couldn't quite figure out. Vandalism seemed wrong and served no purpose now. It was clear that Grayson was planning something. He wasn't sure what, but he had noticed something missing from the list that he thought might be of value. Orbache had taken it upon himself to add to the supplies a handful of cloves of garlic. Better safe than sorry, he assumed. If he was confused about the collection of items, Orbache couldn't even begin to imagine what the cashier must have thought as she checked him out.

At lunch, they all sat and ate quietly. The normally brash and lively group was anything but vibrant now. In truth, most of them were probably having trouble choking down the barely edible sandwiches the guys had slapped together, or perhaps they were just now beginning to really process what was to happen the following evening. They were pushing themselves to the limit on the rink—Lizzy in particular was a rage and pain-filled machine. Up to this point, she had been timid. She had only played in a couple of bouts. Newcomers go through a lengthy training and practice period before even being allowed to play, and most didn't see real action for six months to a year. Roller derby was inherently a dangerous sport, even without vampires to contend with. But today, she looked like a pro. She looked like a woman who had nothing to lose. The necklace with the star charm she had snuck from her sister's corpse rested loosely around her neck.

"She wanted to be an actress," Lizzy looked over and told Veronica as they were eating. Veronica hadn't been able to take her eyes off the necklace that Lizzy kept running her fingers over. "I gave this to her on her eighteenth birthday. I told her she would always be my star," Lizzy said with a bereaved smile. "You were there? You saw it?"

Veronica was sort of caught off guard by the question and had to blink her eyes several times to pull herself out of the trance of the hypnotic little metal medallion. "Yeah, we . . . we were there," she replied quietly.

"I don't need you to tell me she died peacefully," Lizzy stated plainly. "I saw her face. I know that she didn't." She bit her lip, trying to keep her composure. "I just want to know why they picked her," Lizzy wondered, rather than really posing a question Veronica was capable of answering.

"I don't know—" Veronica answered, the only way she knew how.

"I do," said Grayson, who was walking behind them filling up red plastic cups with water from a pitcher, overhearing the question. He placed the pitcher on the table and sat down next to Lizzy, straddling the bench they were sitting on. "It's my fault. It's my fault they chose her," he said, allowing the burden he'd been keeping a secret out into the open.

"How? How is it your fault?" Veronica asked. "Did you even know her?"

Lizzy just stared at him and listened, desperate for whatever he was about to say.

He shook his head. "No, but I put it together earlier, and I'm sure of it now." Grayson knew he had to explain it. "There was this girl. She was with us at the bar the other night. She sat at our table half the night after her friends left early, after happy hour." He had already felt like somewhat of a jerk for his treatment of her at the bar, but now he would bear the weight of her death until his own. "That's the reason they picked her. I'm the reason. She was with me, and that's why they chose her. That's why they killed her. It's because of me," he told her, his voice rattling with sadness.

Lizzy held back tears and smiled. "I actually think she would have been okay with that." Grayson looked at her, not understanding. "She got to hang out with you. She really liked your band. Drinking with you was probably a really big treat for her. Thank you." Lizzy said.

Grayson sat silent for a moment, unable to forget how terrible he had been to the girl, practically ignoring her. He saw no need in sharing that detail. He saw no need in letting Lizzy know he'd barely noticed her sister that night, or that he had seen her as sort of an annoyance. There was no reason to tell her all that. Or telling her that he had no idea what her name was. He couldn't even dignify her humanity by learning her name. That would be a personal hell that Grayson would have to live with. He could only assume she was once a fun, talented girl when she was alive. He was one of the last people to share her company and he hadn't even been able to treat her like a person.

As the late autumn afternoon wore on, Grayson kept an eye on the vanishing daylight hours. At fifteen after five, he motioned to Regina holding up his arm and tapping his wrist. She nodded and signaled for the girls to come off the rink. It was a welcome respite for them, but Regina gave them no time to catch their breath. She instructed them to get their stuff and go straight home—and nowhere else. The sun would be setting soon. The vampires would be awake, and the last thing they needed was to find the entire team here and do away with them before the bout. All their hard work would be for nothing. They had to have the bout. Regina had to get to Bambi, and she had to kill her. It was the only way any of this worked. It was the only way any of them survived.

Quickly gathering their things and escaping through the door, the last remaining daylight hours had never looked more menacing. It was like the end of the day had betrayed the sun. Those twilight hours were working for the night and the creatures that dwelled within it. The sky was grey and cold. Grayson could see his breath as he and Orbache stood in the parking lot watching the girls leave, making sure they made it to their cars and out of sight. Orbache tilted his head up and blew a smoky breath towards the sky.

"Looks like snow," he said.

"Yeah, kind of," Grayson replied, out of habit, rather than actually engaging Orbache's mundane comment.

Orbache looked around as the last of the derby girls left the parking lot, leaving just Regina's green machine and Orbache's vintage, orange Chevy Nova under the flickering lights. They were starting to come on as the evening arrived. He moved the wooden block that had been holding the door open away with his foot and the door slowly and nearly silently swung shut. Grayson looked over at Orbache, saying nothing, but expecting a reason for shutting the door. Orbache reached into his pants pocket, pulled out his car keys and held them out, offering them to Grayson. The little stainless steel

Chevy bowtie keychain caught the light from and glistened like a golden treasure.

"What?" Grayson shrugged his shoulders, not understanding the gesture.

"Leave," Orbache said plainly, almost too quiet to be heard. He looked back, making sure no one inside was listening. "You can leave, you can get out of here, right now," Orbache encouraged. "There is five thousand dollars in the glove box. Take the Nova, take the money. Man, get the hell out of here while you can."

"Why do you have that kind of money sitting in your car?" Grayson asked.

"When I went out earlier, I withdrew some cash," Orbache took Grayson's hand and put the keys in them. "Go, please. You don't have to stay here and die."

"What about them?" Grayson said loudly, pointing inside. He realized his volume and took his voice down to a loud whisper. "I can't just abandon them," he paused, not to think, but to make sure Orbache understood the gravity of his next words. "I'm not going to leave Regina!"

"You're not even together anymore. She broke up with you," Orbache said—not arguing, just stating a fact. Trying desperately to make his friend see his only way out of this unscathed was to not be present when the time came and the shit hit the fan.

"I love her," Grayson said. "It's as simple as that, man. She can hate me, she can date me, she can curse the very air that I breathe, but I love her. And I can't leave her here."

"For God's sake, Grayson, look around you!" He motioned to the dilapidated rink and empty parking lot. "Is this what you are staying for?" Orbache was now yelling at his friend. "You're going to die for this? For her?" Orbache would never have spoken ill of Regina. She was like a sister to him. He had been the third wheel and financier to so many things with the two of them, but when it came down to it, Orbache would have Grayson's back. First and foremost. Always.

Grayson looked at him, his tired greyish blue eyes, sunken in deep pockets of black and blue from a lack of rest. His five o'clock shadow had long since emerged.

"Yeah," Grayson said. "I will."

Orbache wrapped his arms around his friend in a firm embrace. "You're a fucking idiot," Orbache said, his voice nearly being lost in the hood of Grayson's jacket. Letting go of him and standing face to face, he urged, "Take her then. Go, get her now. Go. Just leave."

Grayson looked down at the keys in his hand. They were his ticket to freedom. But instead, he took them and put them in Orbache's coat pocket. Orbache looked on in complete befuddlement.

"I can't. We have to see this through. She can do it. We can win this," Grayson said. "But if you want to go, I'll understand. I don't blame you."

"You know you are making the worst decision of your life right now, don't you?" Orbache told him, running out of steam for trying to convince him to leave.

"Maybe," Grayson admitted with a small smile, realizing it now himself.

"Damn, you're an idiot," Orbache exhaled.

"So, you in or out?" Grayson asked him as he put his key into the lock to get back into the rink. Once he opened the door, there would be no turning back.

"Like there was ever a question," Orbache responded, defeated and resolved to fight the good fight. "I'm in, but if I die, I'm going to haunt you so hard," Orbache said in good spirits, but quite seriously. He was just completely at a loss. He had offered him a way out. And Grayson had politely refused. What Orbache didn't know was that as they were standing in the shadowy light watching the dense fog begin to roll in from the sea wall, Grayson had thought about it. He had wanted to leave. He and Regina could have gotten away. It would've worked, but Grayson couldn't stop thinking about that blonde girl. The one that had lost her life because of him just because she had sat with him at the bar. He would rather be haunted by a friend than by his own soul. He would stay here and help Regina avenge the death of the blonde girl, who against all odds, had remembered the lyrics to his dumb songs and lost her life for it.

Chapter Eighteen
I Saw Your Heart

Grayson locked the door behind him as he and Orbache returned inside from the frigid evening that was surely setting in for the sleepy little coastal village. Grayson always locked the door after closing. It occurred to him, however, that this was the first time that he was locking it with the intent on actually keeping something out. No longer was this a blind precaution—he had seen the danger, and she was real.

Orbache went into the kitchen area and opened the freezer door, staring into it blankly, unimpressed. He sighed, "I hope everyone likes hot dogs." He took several frozen franks out of the freezer and threw them with an echoing clang into a metal pot he had removed from the cabinet above the stove. He filled the pot with water and clicked on the stovetop. The eye burned red as the pot of water came to rest on it. Regina and Veronica, who had both been cleaning up the concession area for no other reason than a distraction, sat down with nothing left to occupy them but their thoughts. The room was quiet—the silence afforded the opportunity to clearly hear themselves think, and the thoughts were dire.

Veronica picked at her fingernails, scraping away the last surviving flecks of violet nail polish from her most recent at-home manicure.

Her nerves were on edge, but this was somehow comforting. Her mind was overflowing with vampires and roller derby and Tabby and now, in this moment of quiet reflection, her mind wandered to Carson. Carson Leightfield, the boyfriend she'd barely spoken to in a week. Just before the guys had returned inside, she had felt the familiar buzz of her phone in her pocket, and she had hit ignore. Again. It was the twelfth time she had done so that day, and each time, the person on the other line was Carson. The genuinely sweet guy, who really did care for her and who she truly had feelings for was now being ignored. Just a few weeks ago, he was the guy who snuck flowers into her gym bag just because. Now, he was a liability. He was a remnant, a scrap of normalcy from a life that no longer existed. A life before vampires. A life before she had been face-to-face with death. Veronica knew she couldn't bring him into this. She could see what the threat of losing Grayson was doing to Regina and to Grayson. She could never do that to Carson. She would have to let him go and maybe, just maybe, when the sun rose on Monday morning, the world would be like it had been before, and she could be waiting on his doorstep with coffee, bagels, and a much overdue apology. That sunrise felt like it was a lifetime away, and deep in her soul, she questioned if she would ever get to see it.

Regina sat opposite from Veronica, twisting the stake in her hand. She kept trying to envision how she was actually going to kill someone. Even someone like Bambi, whom she despised with every part of her mental and physical being. The pale goth bitch had come to town uninvited and without warning began to take away everything Regina cared for: Grayson, Tabby, roller derby, being fucking normal. But as much as she wanted this girl to no longer exist, she didn't know if she had what it took to take a life—even the frail, shadowy ghost of a life. The hollow shell of a person like Bambi was still a person somehow to Regina. She often joked about killing people out of frustration. She had even on more than one occasion threatened to "punch a baby," but for the tough nonchalance she prided herself on portraying to the outside, most if not all of her real physical aggression was reserved exclusively for the rink. She glanced over at Grayson, who had a non-attentive stare directed at her. She smiled at him. He smiled back, seeing her notice that he was halfway staring at her. His smile dropped a little, but he continued to look at her. His pale eyes, glassy and tired, still wanted to look at her, but they were losing an unwinnable battle. Grayson took a deep breath, let his chin rest on his chest, and crossed his arms, finally closing his eyes. Regina could tell he was exhausted. His balled up micro slumber made her realize for the first time just how tired she was. She had pushed herself today far further than she ever thought possible. She had a nagging blister on her right ankle that she chose to ignore, and her elbow was aching, but in the grand scheme of things, she could deal with it. She was still alive. That was an achievement that couldn't be overstated at the moment. She stretched her back and rolled her head between her shoulders several times, unable to loosen the tension she was holding in her muscles.

"I'm going to go take a bath. Save me a hotdog," Regina said, stretching again as she stood up. She walked to the back unevenly, her whole body now aching. She had finally stopped long enough to sit down, and now she was feeling the ramifications of the day.

Grayson stirred enough to look over as she left. He didn't like her going anywhere by herself—not now, not after the sun had set. He guessed though that a bath was the exception. His eyes beginning to water, he closed them again. It was the culmination of his exhaustion, and he was finally beginning to agree that maybe Regina had been right in breaking up with him. This was the first time that he had shown so much concern for her in the entire six year span of their relationship. He cared about her, he always had, but he had taken her independence for granted. He had never felt like she needed that reassurance that he loved her. They had never been that couple—overly needy, dependent on the other to feel complete. It was only in these last few days that he realized how incomplete he actually was without her.

Regina sat on the edge of the small clawfoot tub that was in the bathroom in Grayson's living area within the rink. She loved the little antique bath. Grayson had surprised her with it during renovations when he was preparing to move into the rink permanently. He had told her that he wanted to make sure she could have a proper bath when she stayed the night, or if she wanted to move in with him. Regina had been horrified at the thought of living with Grayson at the roller rink. She'd sidestepped answering by gushing over the tub. He'd never brought it up again, and she'd kept her own place all these years. Regina pulled the shower curtain to one side and turned on the water, letting it run over her hands as it warmed. It was refreshing—she rubbed her finger underneath the water rinsing dried blood from one of her cuticles. She had rammed her hand into one of the girls' pads earlier in the day. It had drawn blood, but it was minimal. The water finally reached a steady heat, and she stopped the drain for it to begin to fill. She stood up from the edge of the tub, stepping over to the counter and looking in the mirror. She laughed at herself a little. Right now, she was indeed the epitome of a hot mess. Her normally well-shaped hair, braided up on the sides with a semi-frohawk on top, was mashed and misshapen from the helmet. She had put on no makeup today, and she could see a bruise forming over her right eye. Regina had been reckless out there, but she felt like if there was ever a time to throw caution to the wind, now would be it.

Regina began to undress as the hot water connected with the cool air in the small bathroom, filling it with steam. Not bothering to fold her clothes, she left them bunched up on the floor where they fell. She turned off the faucet and slid into the hot bathwater, letting it consume and overwhelm her. It was like she'd been given fresh life, reborn. She closed her eyes and let the world fade away with a deep relaxing sigh. There was peace, if only for a minute.

When Regina did finally reopen her eyes, she glanced over at the mirror, which was now covered in condensation. In the corner, there was a little hand-drawn heart. She traced it in the air with her finger. She had drawn that heart weeks ago while Grayson was showering. Regina ignored the fact that clearly he had not cleaned the bathroom since they had split up. Quietly sneaking in the bathroom and silently sending a love note that he never even noticed. If he had noticed, he never mentioned it.

A knock at the door startled her out of her daydream.

"The door is unlocked," Regina said, a little annoyed that her bath was being disturbed. Even more so because it was probably Orbache, too impatient to wait to pee, or too stupid or too good to use the public restrooms in the front. She had her hand on the shower curtain, ready to pull it closed when he came in. Her wet body was the last thing that guy was getting an eyeful of.

"Just checking to make sure you're okay in there," Grayson's voice called through the door, surprised she was just going to let him come in.

Regina felt a little embarrassed. "Yes, I'm fine," she replied sweetly, though a little pestered that she was being babysat. "We're all still in the same building, Grayson. I'll be fine," she said, mocking his newly discovered overprotective demeanor.

"Yeah, I know. I'm sorry—I'll let you get back to your bath," Grayson said, touching the door gently with his fingers as he went to leave.

"You know, you should really clean your bathroom," Regina jokingly chided him, enjoying being able to talk to him again about something other than vampires.

Grayson pulled his hand back, sportingly defensive. "I did! That bathroom is clean, woman," he said playfully.

"I know you haven't cleaned this bathroom in like three weeks, Grayson Hines," Regina said, certain she knew something Grayson didn't and ready to call him out on it.

"How so?" Grayson asked, less than curious about her concern in the cleanliness of his bathroom, but absolutely engaged in the banter.

Regina smiled as she sat up in the bathtub, hoping her flirtations weren't being filtered out through the bathroom door. "I drew a little heart on the mirror that you didn't know about," she revealed—her gotcha moment. "And it's still there, so I know you haven't cleaned the bathroom since I left." She sat back with a certain pleasure in being right. He was quiet on the other side. She had him—winner

winner.. Her victory was short-lived. Grayson knew something she didn't.

"I did see your heart, Regina," he said, leaning up against the door a little.

He was so quiet, Regina leaned forward a little, wondering if he was still out there. Had she hurt his feelings? She really hadn't meant to. She went to apologize, but he spoke before she was able.

"Your heart was on the other side of the mirror," he replied. "That one was mine back to you." His crooked grin stretched across his face. Regina could feel it even through the inch and a half of the thick wooden door. She scrunched her face a little and looked up at the mirror and saw that he was right. She had drawn her heart on the left corner with the handle to the medicine cabinet, she remembered now. She had purposely put it there so she was certain he would see it.

"I never saw this," she said to him through the door, a little surprised and more than slightly charmed.

"Yeah, I know," Grayson said, with a bit of sadness. "You never came back." There was a short pause. "Hey, dinner is ready when you are done."

She sat silently in the tub, trying to gather her thoughts. Everything she wanted to say was running through her mind in a million different directions. Regina called out his name, but there was no response. She called out again a little louder, to make sure she gave him every chance to hear her. "Grayson? Grayson, you still out there?" she asked with no response. She brought her knee up in the tub and rested her chin on it, her head turned to stare at the little condensation heart. The water was now beginning to cool, giving her cause to stand up. Grabbing her towel, she stepped out of the tub and onto the little tan, woven rug. Regina walked over and traced the heart over with her finger. *This one is mine back to you,* she thought with a smile.

Chapter Nineteen
Playing With Their Food

Following a less than satisfying meal of lukewarm, boiled hotdogs and off-brand nacho cheese triangle tortilla chips, they sat around the table for a few minutes before heading back to Grayson's living area and barricading themselves in the bedroom again. Their time at the table hadn't been silent, but for the life of them, not a single one of them could even remember what they discussed. They flipped on the small TV in Grayson's room, clicking around and trying to avoid the local news stations. The last thing they needed now was more bad news. They flipped through the channels until they found an unseasonably early pre-Thanksgiving showing of *Miracle on 34th Street* that was just starting. It was the 1947 version of the film—it had been remastered and cleaned up, but there was still something so timeless about the black and white movie. Veronica, who had been controlling the remote from the floor where she was laying near the small space heater, stopped on the movie.

"We could use a miracle right now," she said. No one argued. She put the remote on the floor in front of her and pulled the wool blanket she had up over her arms. It wasn't long before she fell asleep. Orbache, who normally would've been the one to criticize the choice of movie, was already asleep sitting propped up against the wall. Regina slowly got up from the floor where she had been sitting and grabbed a small knit throw, covering Orbache up with it. She walked back over to her spot on the floor and prepared to sit down when Grayson silently patted the spot beside him on the bed and motioned for her to join him. Regina climbed onto the bed without question, sliding down beside him and wrapping her arms around him with a deep and freeing sigh. They watched the movie together in the soft glow, away from the vampires, away from the past. At that moment, it was just the two of them and the movie, and that in itself was a miracle enough.

Regina watched the movie—really watching it for the first time since she was a child. She realized how much she had missed the real message of the movie so many times before. She always took for granted that the miracle was that Edmund Gwenn's Kris Kringle made it out of the asylum in time for Christmas, because he was the real Santa. He had to be out in time for Christmas. But what everyone in that movie really got was hope. They were each given their own miracle. Maureen O'Hara's character got the miracle of belief—to believe in the impossible and anything could happen. She found love. She found a family. And she found happiness. Hell, she even got a house out of the whole deal.

Regina saw herself as a lot like Maureen O'Hara. She definitely needed a miracle. And it was as simple as that. Regina just had to believe if she wanted to find happiness. She said a short prayer as she closed her heavy eyes and drifted to sleep, her head nuzzled on

Grayson's chest. The musically rhythmic beating of his heart sent her into a dreamless sleep. No dreams were better than nightmares.

Grayson looked down at Regina, asleep and embracing him in a way he had not experienced in weeks. He leaned forward ever so slightly and inhaled her scent. Her hair smelled faintly of honey. It was nice.

He propped himself up where the corner of the bed and the wall met. He was determined to stay awake and keep guard. Everyone he had left to care about in this life was in this room. Veronica and Orbache, were here in this room. Regina. The person who he loved most slept next to him. He resigned himself to protect them all at whatever cost. Grayson had lost so many people over the course of his relatively young life. He had become accustomed to loss, but he refused to lose what he had right there laying next to him. He could sleep when he was dead. Grayson pushed that thought out of his head, hoping that his mind wandering would not prove to be prophetic. He sat up, watching the movie and listening to the soft sounds of those sleeping around him. He did his best, but before he knew it, exhaustion finally grabbed a hold of him. He could feel his eyelids getting heavy. He tried to shake it off—he fought to stay awake, to keep guard, but it was no use. His eyes closed and he slept.

Their peaceful slumber was interrupted with a crash and the sounds of shattering of glass. The room awoke in an instant. Regina rolled off the bed and grasped at air, trying to find the stake she'd left on the floor. The little green digits glowing on the alarm clock behind her read 3:25 a.m. Grayson gripped the baseball bat in his hand and moved the chest of drawers from in front of the door. He cautiously exited the room. He was followed closely behind by Orbache, who had smartly grabbed a flashlight to help lead the way, tapping the clove of garlic in his pocket gently—like a silent prayer to seasoning. Regina and Veronica brought up the rear. They all cautiously reached the front of the building to the source of the commotion. The front door was shattered. A brick with paper tied around it lay on the floor, surrounded by glass. It was clear it had been used as a projectile, but it also held a message. Regina quickly stepped over and picked it up, careful not to let her bare feet connect to the shards of glass. She ripped the paper off, reading the scribbled note. She turned back to the others.

"So much for the home-field advantage," she said, preparing to read the note aloud. But as she turned to face them, they stared past her into the abyss.

Veronica pointed, her movements shaky. She stuck her hand out ahead of her, motioning behind Regina.

"Regina."

Her name was all she said as she stared into the distance, her voice full of fear. It was all she could manage. Veronica's eyes were wide, her mouth slightly agape. Regina turned around slowly to see for herself what had nabbed Veronica and the boys' attention so terrifyingly. As it came into view, a cold chill shot down her spine—but not from the icy night air flooding in from the broken glass door. No, it was what she saw. It was the visage of spectres watching them from the fog-riddled parking lot. Illuminated only slightly by the street lights stood a dark figure. Regina recognized the silhouette—it was Bambi. The vampire queen was flanked by ten other dark, menacing figures. No words were spoken. They made no movements. They stood and stared inside at them. Regina suddenly felt like every lobster she'd ever looked at in the tank. Being watched by those who controlled her fate. Regina couldn't see their eyes, but she knew they were watching her, waiting for her to do something. Maybe they were hoping she would run out there and threaten to fight them right here, right now. Then they would just drop her to her knees and bleed her out. She had no plans to wither away. Regina stood firm, feeling Bambi's eyes on her, sizing her up, mulling over the amount of a threat she was actually going to pose. Regina smiled at her. She knew she could see it, and she knew she would hate it. The smile was now the only thing hiding the truth. Regina was in over her head. The fog grew thicker, and it seemed to engulf them. They were gone, vanished into the mist. The parking lot was still hauntingly grim and ominous, once again only occupied by the two cars, the fog, and now fear.

Regina turned back around, the paper crumpled in her fist.

"Midnight. The shipping yards. That's where we play them," Regina said. "That's where I kill them." She stepped over the glass and walked away, throwing the paper into the trash can as she passed it.

"Regina!" Grayson called loudly, feeling like there should be more of a discussion about what had just occurred.

She turned around briefly. "I don't want to talk about it, I want to go back to bed," Regina replied firmly. "There is nothing we can do now. We wait until tomorrow. We wait until midnight. They made it perfectly clear that the ball is in their court. I will play their game. And I'm going to win it." She turned back around and walked away, squeezing back through the door and dresser to get back into Grayson's bedroom.

Grayson ran ahead of Veronica and Orbache and entered his room. Regina had already climbed into the bed, covered head to toe with the quilt and facing the wall, away from him.

"Regina," he called to her, his tender voice willing her to talk to him, knowing she needed to talk to him.

She replied from under the quilt, a blanket of protection. She refused to look at him. "I just want to go to sleep. Please don't make me talk about it." Regina's voice cracked. "Please just let me go back to sleep."

Grayson got the message. He could sense that he shouldn't push the issue further. He decided to do the one thing he knew he could: he would just be there for her. Just be there *with* her. He climbed into the bed next to her and put his arms around her, finding her hand somewhere in the tangled mess of covers and holding it, fingers intertwined. "Go back to sleep," he whispered sweetly into her ear.

Back out in the foyer, Veronica was trying to sweep up the broken glass with half a broom. Orbache was coming in from the storeroom with a large piece of black plastic and duct tape to put over the hole in the glass. Veronica held up the broken broom as if to question him.

"Yeah, Grayson used it to make the stake," Orbache replied, explaining the now impossibly difficult to use broom.

She nodded in amused understanding.

"Hey, forget it. We can clean it up in the morning," Orbache finally said after watching her try to squat and maneuver half a broom. "Go back to bed," he gently encouraged.

Veronica was pleasantly surprised by the gesture and the tone of his voice. In all the years she had known him, this may have only been the second time he'd expressed any sense of compassion for anyone other than himself. She smiled and nodded, propping the broom up against the wall and watching it slide down and onto the floor. She began walking back to the room as Orbache shut the lights back off as they went. Veronica paused, glancing into the garbage can where Regina had thrown the crumpled note from the vampires away. Veronica realized it wasn't just a note. Veronica saw what Regina had not wanted them to see, why she had thrown the note away instead of letting them all see it. The paper wrapping the brick had not been blank, but it was an inkjet printout of a scanned polaroid photo. A bloody and beaten Tabitha. Her eyes nearly swollen shut. Her lips were cracked and bloody, split and grey, starved for moisture. Veronica reached in and picked it up to see the full scope. At the bottom was a handwritten caption.

"Playing with our food."

It included a small smiley face with fangs drawn onto the crescent-shaped smile.

Veronica turned it over, and there were the bout instructions. Indeed, it was to be midnight at the shipping yards, near freight station 12 at the end of the dock. She quickly threw the photo back into the trash as Orbache approached from behind her.

"Something wrong?" he asked, looking at her.

She shook her head, "Nope, same ol', same ol'. Vampires and such," she said quickly, stalling, trying to come up with something better. "I was just waiting on you. You know Grayson will flip out if we don't stay in pairs." She laughed it off.

"Right," Orbache said, convinced something was up, but too tired to put much thought into it.

Veronica was grateful he had bought the haphazard excuse. He turned the lights off and guided them back to the bedroom with the flashlight. They walked in the door, and Grayson turned, putting his finger to his lips and asking them to be quiet.

Veronica understood—she now knew exactly why Regina had just wanted to go back to sleep. Veronica curled back up on the floor. The lights went off, and the room grew quiet once again. Veronica folded her arms under an old, thin pillow Grayson had found in the closet and given her to sleep on. She propped herself up, staring at the little red light on the stereo. She was too wired to immediately go back to sleep, her adrenaline still pumping from being startled awake by the shattering glass. She wasn't sure if she would ever forget the sight of the Bloody Mother Suckers lurking in the fog. And then there was Tabby. Tabby was an innocent pawn in all of this. She had done nothing but be friends with Regina. Veronica imagined that this must have been how Grayson felt his role in the death of the blonde girl. How could you not hold yourself responsible for something like that? It was at no direct fault of your own, and yet it was completely because of you. Veronica had sort of overlooked how Regina must have been feeling, what with the hell that these past few days had been. Her hands were stained with the blood of the dead. She was damned, no matter her course of action. Veronica closed her eyes, wanting nothing more than for this all to be over—wanting it all to go away. In the back of her mind, she knew that the worst was yet to come. The sun would rise tomorrow, the sun would set tomorrow, and then they would all have to fight for their lives.

Chapter Twenty
Gone

It was before daybreak when Grayson woke up. The sun hadn't yet begun its slow climb skyward. The urgent need to relieve himself forced him from sleep. He slid out of the bed and went to the bathroom, aiming for the side of the toilet bowl in an attempt to pee as quietly as possible, not wanting to wake anyone. Afterward, he walked back into the room and looked around. Regina was still sleeping in his bed. He saw her there, just like that so many times before. Her hand tucked tightly beneath her chin, the covers hugging her curves. His only hope was to one day see her there again. He slid past Orbache, who was asleep posted up next to the door frame. Grayson carefully bent down, reaching into Orbache's coat pocket and fishing out the car keys, gingerly clutching the metal in his fist before it could make a sound. Orbache hadn't even stirred. He was none the wiser. Grayson stepped over Veronica, asleep on the floor, and pushed the chest of drawers out of the doorway just enough for him to inch out without making a sound. He slipped out of the room, turning briefly and taking one last look at Regina before closing the door behind him. He knew that to keep her forever, this was the only way. It had to be this way. It had to be now. It was his last chance. And he knew it.

He walked out into the concession area, grabbed his coat off the back of a chair, threw his arms into the sleeves, and pulled it tight. Grayson exited the rink, and seconds later, the robust engine sound of the classic Nova rattled away from the rink. The rink was quiet. Grayson was gone.

Chapter Twenty-One
Making Plans

There was no alarm set for this morning. At some point well after dawn, Orbache had jolted himself awake, brushing invisible ants from his arms and legs. It was a recurring stress dream he was grateful no one had witnessed. He dusted off the last bits of the dream lingering in his mind as he stretched out his legs. Orbache looked over and saw the chest had been moved and was suddenly very awake, immediately aware something was wrong. He jumped up, nearly stumbling over Veronica asleep on the floor, cocooned in blankets. The noise of this caused her to wake up just as Orbache went out the door, calling for Grayson in the dimly lit rink. Suddenly, the thought occurred to him. His keys. He patted his breast pocket, realizing what he already suspected. The car keys were gone. Regina, who had also woken up amidst the confusion, came out of the room, followed closely in tow by Veronica.

Orbache saw her, and panic ran through him. He tried to hide it, but he knew his face was betraying him. He was the one who had put the idea of leaving in Grayson's head in the first place. It was his car, his keys, his money. It was his plan—Orbache had given Grayson the means to leave, and he had.

"Where's Grayson?" she asked, still sleepily and surprisingly showing no real sense of alarm.

Orbache was still processing the facts, his hands on his head, awkwardly stomping around in circles. "He's gone," he said before he even really realized the words were leaving his mouth. "He left." Somehow saying it out loud made it real.

For Regina, now the alarms were now sounding loud and clear. She felt the blood rush to her face. "What do you mean?" she asked. "What do you mean he's gone?"

A million different scenarios of the same design ran through her mind. Had the vampires come in the night and stolen him? Was he dead, lying in the cold somewhere, his corpse frozen in the frost? Was his little scruffy beard frozen solid, his eyes never to open again? Or worse—was he now one of them? Destined to be away from her for eternity? She couldn't stand the thought of it.

"I don't understand," Orbache said, more to himself than anyone else. "He said he wouldn't."

Regina was annoyed and concerned and half asleep. A dangerous combination. "What do you mean he said he wouldn't?" She was starting to comprehend that perhaps Grayson had fled on his own accord. "James, where is Grayson?" Regina asked, forcefully stepping in closer to him. Orbache rarely heard his first name, and it sent a disagreeable twinge through his body. He was in trouble, and he knew it. He honestly wasn't sure if Regina was going to hit him or not, so he spilled his guts like a busted piñata. He was getting really good at telling Regina things he probably shouldn't.

"He took my car, and he left. Regina, he's gone," Orbache said sympathetically. "I told him last night he should just leave, and I guess he took the opportunity—but he said he wouldn't. He told me wouldn't." Orbache paused. "He said he couldn't leave without you."

Regina's legs began to give way. She no longer had the power to keep upright, and she slid into a nearby chair with a thud. She was nearly hyperventilating. She was in shock. She was hurt and alone. She felt the tears forming in her eyes.

"I'm so sorry," Orbache said. "He said he wouldn't leave without you. I swear."

Grayson, ever the master of timing, chose that moment to enter through the door of the rink with a plastic bag in hand. The black plastic covering the broken glass panel in the door frame caught the gust from the door opening and made a loud popping and slapping noise, catching everyone's attention. Grayson was as caught off guard as this by anyone. He had honestly hoped that he would have been able to sneak back in unnoticed. That was definitely not the case.

Regina stood up and ran over to him. She was elated and infuriated in the same breath. He immediately saw the worry and concern, the joy and anger in her face. He looked at her, confused.

"What?" he asked her, looking over at Orbache for clarification, but it was clear that Orbache was just as surprised to see him as Regina. "I went and got us all breakfast," Grayson said, not completely understanding the tension in the room. "Is something going on?"

"I thought you were gone. I thought you had left—" Regina's voice was becoming shaky. It crackled as the emotion boiled its way to the surface. She was fighting tears. "I thought you had left without me," she said, no longer able to keep the tears from flowing, no longer able to hide that the thought of him leaving her behind had broken her heart. Her face scrunched, and she fanned her eyes, almost embarrassed that she was crying.

Grayson looked at her, standing in front of him crying. He wanted nothing more than to never see her cry again. He just wanted to make her happy. To love her, and be loved in return. Grayson was done halfassing whatever life he had left. He cast away second thoughts, ignoring the fact that he knew better than what he was about to do. Rational thought left him, and he succumbed to the moment.

"Regina, I'm not going anywhere without you," he said, stepping forward, dropping the plastic bag to the ground, its contents no longer a concern to him. Grayson took his thumb and wiped the tears from face, and leaned down into her, and she instinctively rose to her tiptoes to meet him. She couldn't have fought the moment even if she wanted to.. His hands slid down her sides and wrapped around her waist. Their lips met in such a way she had never experienced. Every thought, every impulse, every nerve ending tingled. The moment was electric. His skin was still cool from the winter outside, and it melted into her warm and flushed face. Regina's arms made their way around him, under his coat, resting between the cool lining of the jacket and the thin jersey of his shirt. She could feel the warmth of his skin through the fabric. Regina opened her eyes pulling back from him. Grayson wiped the residual tears from her face, and kissed her again, short and sweetly.

"Never. I will never go anywhere without you. I promise you that," he told her again in a way she had no choice but to believe him, because she knew he meant it. She stared in his eyes. They were glassy with moisture. The pale grey blues of his eyes were small oceans that captivated her gaze as if it was the first time she had ever set her eyes upon his. They stood there, and no words were spoken. They held onto each other, afraid to let go.

Orbache, who was standing off to the side watching happily uncomfortably, glanced from the two still embracing over to

Veronica, hoping for a sympathetic understanding glance, of "what the hell just happened." Instead, she was eating it up with a spoon. Veronica was nearly weeping out of joy, like this was her own personal Nicholas Sparks novel. She had a grin stretched across her face and was flapping her happy hands. Orbach was just inherently befuddled. He was happy they had *worked things out?* Just not right in front of him.

"So, was that breakfast for all of us you just threw on the floor?" he asked, giving up on understanding anything anymore.

Grayson, smiling and still holding Regina, replied, "Yeah, I got pancakes." He kissed Regina again and pulled away from her, bending down and picking up the bag.

"I thought we could use something a little better than boiled hotdogs," Grayson said. He set the bag up on the countertop and pulled out two styrofoam containers—no worse for wear from their trip to the ground. Grayson set out several plastic forks and they gathered around the counter to eat, not bothering to take the time for plates scraping margarine from little round containers, pouring syrup liberally, and eating straight from the containers. It was amazing what power food could have. It was warm and sweet and delicious—they couldn't have asked for a better breakfast.

Regina was so pleasantly surprised that Grayson had gone and gotten breakfast. He had only done that a handful of times that she could remember. Thinking about it, she could actually count the times on one hand—not just a turn of phrase.. And in this case, it was just as impactful as the moment when she assumed he had left her was.

The group ate happily, but Grayson had actually lucked out. He had only gotten the idea at the last minute to pick up breakfast. He had been rounding the corner on the road back to the rink and realized he had been gone longer than he had anticipated. He decided to cover his tracks, so he had stopped at Take-O's, the 24-hour breakfast joint a block away. Grayson was infinitely grateful now that he had grabbed the last minute diversion. He took the car keys from his pocket and slid them across the counter to Orbache.

Grayson had actually snuck out that morning to accomplish something completely different. He smiled to himself, knowing he had succeeded with the deception, and no one was any the wiser. Grayson took a bite of syrup-drenched pancake and plotted his next move.

Chapter Twenty-Two
Handful of Fools

Unfortunately for Regina and Grayson, there was little time to enjoy this brief reconciliation, or relapse, or whatever had just taken place. Regina had slowly tried to slide her hand into the front Grayson's jeans, obstructed from the others' view by the counter, hoping they would have a few minutes to rekindle in the back room. But he had diverted the attempt as a couple of roller derby girls started showing up as they had been instructed, right on time. Just before 8 a.m., Lizzy arrived first. Grayson handed her his fork and told her to eat as he excused himself to go change clothes. Orbache left the table himself shortly after Grayson, carefully stuffing a receipt from the plastic bag into his pocket. He was hoping no one had seen the covert move. He pushed open the door as Grayson was standing in the middle of the room taking off the ratty softball jersey he had been wearing the last couple of days, not caring or even thinking to change it. Orbache propped himself up in the doorframe and crossed his arms, staring intently at Grayson with a raised eyebrow heavily implying he knew something. Grayson shot back a confused glance as he reached over and opened one of the middle drawers of the chest that was awkwardly still out of place in the room, still not having been returned to its typical location against the wall after being used to barricade the door. He snagged another t-shirt from the drawer and threw it over his head. Orbache looked behind him, making sure no one was coming and stepped into the room. He silently shut the door behind him.

"What's up?" Grayson asked, knowing Orbache had something to say and was growing impatient with the build up.

"Where did you go?" Orbache asked, his tone reinforcing to Grayson that he now knew conclusively that buying breakfast wasn't his sole purpose for leaving.

"To get breakfast," Grayson said as he pulled on his shirt and attempted to step toward the door. Orbache reached out and stopped him, blocking his path. Orbache was done with not being in on the plans. He was fed up with the secrecy.

"Why don't you just tell me where you went?" Orbache pressed, annoyed that Grayson wouldn't come clean. "I found the receipt in the bag. That place is less than a block away, and you hate driving." Orbache had toured in a small van with Grayson for years, being forced to listen to his bitching and moaning about the car rides. "You've walked to that place forty-five times in the last six months. There is no way you would take the car for that." Orbache was on the verge of angrily begging. "So, why don't you just tell me where you went?"

Orbache was angry he had been thrown into the middle of a vampire epidemic, his life was on the line, and now he wasn't getting full disclosure about a shopping trip.

Grayson looked at him, fearing he was about to have to come clean, but not fully prepared to divulge the secret he was keeping, when Orbache gave him an out. Without even knowing it, Orbache had helped him keep his deceit a little longer.

"Is it about that secret list of stuff you had me go buy yesterday?" Orbache questioned him again impatiently. "Is it, Grayson? Cause I'm tired of not knowing what the fuck is going on around here!"

Grayson sighed, faking his aversion to coming clean, as it were. "Yes, okay. I have a plan," Grayson faked admission. "I just didn't want the girls finding out about it yet."

Orbache relaxed his posture a little, still listening intently.

"I did some research about killing vampires, their weaknesses," Grayson continued. "I didn't want to tell them too early, because I was afraid if I said anything yesterday and the vampires got a hold of them, they might let it slip about our plans or how much we knew about their weaknesses."

What Grayson was saying was the truth—just the truth of why he had hidden the stuff on his secret list. He hadn't wanted the girls to know about that, in the event that one or more of them were kidnapped. The less they knew, the better for everyone. That was all true. It was a lie that it had anything to do with his mission this morning. However, it seemed like enough information to calm Orbache, as his arms relaxed and his jawline softened.

"Damn, man—that's all you had to say. You don't have to be so secretive. I'm not mad at you, though. I understand now. That was probably smart. The less people in the know, the better," Orbache said, accepting it at face value. "I just want to be one of the ones in the know from now on, okay?"

Grayson felt genuinely guilty about lying to his friend like that. Orbache trusted him. Grayson had never given him a reason not to. It hurt him to have done it, but right now he didn't have the time to go into the lengthy discussion that would have definitely ensued if Orbache knew where he had really gone that morning just before dawn.

Back in the main area of the rink, six of the girls had arrived and were picking at the remains of the pancakes like vultures who had found the last scraps of carrion on the side of the road. Regina nervously checked the wall clock repeatedly. She was trying not to show concern at the minimal number of girls who had shown up to this point. A few more girls arrived, and at nearly a quarter until nine, there were a total of twelve girls including Regina and Veronica. About that time, Abby and another girl Holly arrived through the door, checking out the broken window as they entered, sharing a glance that was clearly reflective of an ongoing conversation.

"Hey, girls," Regina said, greeting them half-heartedly. Her mind was elsewhere—she was trying to figure out where her team had vanished to. She was afraid to draw attention to the matter, convinced that if she ignored it, maybe it would go away. She finally said it aloud as the small group were getting geared up.

"Where is everybody?" Regina asked, defeated. She had been riding high from the display of solidarity the day before.

There was an uncomfortable silence as the girls all shared glances, no one wanting to be the bearer of bad news. Abby's voice rippled through the stagnant conversation. "They're not coming," Abby admitted. She was sad to have to break the news of dissension in the ranks to Regina. Abby had been on the team for a few years. She had even once been co-captain under Regina, but had to cut back her duties after getting married. "Abby-bliterate" was what she was called on the rink. She was naturally a dirty blonde who had dyed her hair so many times it looked dry and brittle. She was actually younger than Regina, but her hair and caked on makeup aged her. Abby regularly wore her purpley grey hair in two braided pigtails, which would flap out the sides of her helmet. She had once gotten a penalty for slapping a girl in the face with her pigtail during a jam. She squatted, propping herself up on her knees. She looked at Regina, waiting for her next move. They all looked to Regina.

Regina was still processing the words. It was exactly what she feared. "What do you mean? Why?"

Abby shifted her weight, rocking on her heels. "Look, a bunch of us met up this morning for breakfast to talk about all of this, Regina," Abby said, clearing the air. "They ran a special on the news last night about your sister," she looked over and acknowledged Lizzy, "and that Harrington guy," referring to Greg, "and, well, damn Regina—we all sort of realized that this was real." She said it very matter of fact. "I mean, I don't know what we thought, but . . . but this is real—like *people are dying* real." She rocked forward, standing up. She was gesturing too wildly with her hands to stay seated. "And a lot of the girls said they just couldn't do it. I tried—girl, you know I have your back. I'm telling you, I tried." Her devotion was not in question. "I mean, everybody is still super supportive, and they all want you to win, but they're scared, Regina. I'm sorry, but we're all you've got, babe."

Regina looked around. The overwhelming support of the girls the day before had been too good to be true. She'd known it deep down. Some united front she had. What was once a mighty force, a solid group of thirty-three amazing female warriors fighting behind her had dwindled to a handful of fools following Regina to the brink of death. Regina sunk into a grey folding chair and folded over with her head in her hands, feeling defeated.

"Nah, nu-uh," Abby called over to her. "Get back up, girl. We're here for you! May not be many of us, but we're here."

"Yeah—look, Regina, we have fourteen girls," Veronica joined in, trying to rally Regina. "That is enough to fill out the roster. We have enough." It would be tight, but Veronica was right. "Would be nice to have some alternates, sure, but they're vampires. I'm not even certain how much they are going to be sticklers for regulations." Veronica smiled, trying to lighten the mood and bring her friend back from the edge—and for once, she was doing an exceptionally good job.

"She's right, Regina. We have enough people. We're here with you," Lizzy said. "We came back for you. We didn't give up on you, so don't give up on us. We're all here for you."

"Don't give up on *Tabby*." Veronica added, leaning in close to her and putting her hand on her shoulder.

Regina sat back up—resolved, renewed, and focused. "You're right," she said with forced gusto. "We have all we need here. We can do this." She took a deep breath and stood up. "Are you ready, girls? Let's get out on the rink."

Regina shook it off. Maybe she needed that brief moment of disbelief in herself. Maybe the girls weren't supposed to show up. Maybe it was fate being on her side. If they had shown up, maybe she would've been too confident—too certain of their chances of success. That definitely wasn't the case now. This made it real again. This brought her back to a place where she was the underdog. And the underdog always pulled it out in the end. Right? She could only hope at this point. Regina had not been the underdog in a long time when it came to derby. They were the team that the other teams dreaded to see on the schedule. Regina had gleefully led her team to crush the dreams of a lot of underdogs over the years. She hoped she was not about to have a bitter mouthful of her own medicine.

Regina stuffed her foot into her skate, catching her breath as the blister she had forgotten about scraped the side of the skate. She cringed but let it go. Blisters heal. She let out a slow deep breath and forced her foot fully into the boot of the skate, lacing it up. She repeated over her plan for the day in her head. Regina intended to let the girls go at about two in the afternoon. They would practice through lunch. She would give them the chance to go home and eat, offering them time to sleep before they had to meet back up at the docks. Regina knew it was foolish to think that anyone would actually be able to manage to sleep before the bout, but she would at least give them the option. They deserved it. They were working so hard. And they deserved the chance to say goodbye to their families, just in case.

Chapter Twenty-Three
A Change in the Ranks

The eight-wheeled, seemingly bionic mavens circled the track like greyhounds, blindly running after their faux long-eared bait. Weaving in and out of the others, throwing themselves into their opponents. The rattling and clicking sound of the skates hit the track was reminiscent of a cacophony of frogs on a muggy summer evening. Once again, Lizzy was blazing up the track. Around her neck, she still wore her pendant of revenge, the little star charm necklace. The necklace that until recently belonged to her sister, the girl that had been bludgeoned and bled at the hands of the vampires. The timer sounded at the end of the jam, one of many times the team had already scrimmaged that morning. Veronica wheeled off to the side to catch her breath.

Veronica was running herself bare, playing hard. It was beginning to get the better of her. Regina rolled over to her and put her hand on her back as she bent over—encouraging, comforting. Regina's presence was reassuring, but the physical toll she was taking on herself was almost too much. Hands on her thighs, breathing deep and slow, Veronica tried not to vomit from exertion. She felt like her lungs were expanding to hit her stomach. It was risky just to breathe. She wiped the sweat from her face as she looked up to see Regina skating back over to the group. Watching the sweat drip from her face to the floor, she tried to control the saliva in her mouth threatening to prepare the way for the reemergence of her breakfast. Veronica sighed as she finally caught her breath and felt confident enough to stand up from her bent over stance. She had made up her mind during the short respite. She was certain of what her next move should be. Now, she just had to find the right moment to break the news to Regina.

The afternoon wore on, and tensions ran thin. As planned, Regina sent the girls home early. She sent them away in the hopes that they would return, but not overly confident of anyone actually going through with it. Would any of them even show up? Would a single player show up and see it through with her to the end? She and Veronica had even left the rink for a few hours, much to Grayson's disapproval. He had not liked that idea, but they assured him they would be back before sunset. Regina didn't really understand his concern—if they were going to kill her before the match, they could have just done it already. This was just a game to them. Regina assured him they were just going to pick up a few things and that if he kept them locked up in the rink any longer, she might go crazy. He had begrudgingly agreed to the idea. Regina had played it off, but she truly did feel a little bad about pushing the issue so forcefully. She had not been completely honest with Grayson when she had told him that they were just heading home to grab a few things. She and Veronica were going to go home, but they had another stop first. She needed to see it with her own eyes. She needed to see it before tonight. Regina wanted to be prepared. She never liked walking into any situation blind. At least she could see it. No surprises.

The green machine bolted from the asphalt county service road and hit a private gravel drive. Attling along parallel to the never ending chain-link fence and counting down signs, she barrelled up on the one with a large and faded number twelve in black block lettering on the dusty, sun-bleached orange metal sign. This was it. Regina hit the brakes with force, kicking up a cloud of dirt and debris. She slammed the car into park. As the dust settled, they could see the water at the harbor through the windshield. Grey and choppy, the sea was as uneasy about everything as they were. Several gulls and a rogue pigeon hopped and screeched on the ground as they stepped out of the car, picking whatever scraps they could find in the small rocks—the last remnants of when this was a bustling industrial park. Generations of animals that refused to see the writing on the wall, destined to die after a meager existence because they refused to fly away. The gravel crunched under the girls' feet as they walked out onto the wharf through a large gap in the fragmented remains of the now obsolete security fence. The gate by the guard tower had merely been dummy-locked. Everyone had left this place to die—except for those birds. The sea air hit them, the salty smell of the water and the faint hint of machine oil and fish. Regina looked around and saw the building with the corresponding orange sign with the blocked, black number twelve.

People rarely ever came down this far into the yards anymore —actual business on these docks was a thing of the past. Six or seven years ago, when importing and exporting was a booming industry, they had expanded the shipping yards from eight freight stations to twelve. They had even begun the environmental impact studies on dredging and digging the shipping lanes deeper for larger freight. It was a political move to show how robust capitalism could be in the more rural areas just outside the tourist-heavy coastal towns. As it turns out though, capitalism was the result of tourism and not the other way around. In the last few years, the economy had taken a nosedive nationally and, even more evident, locally. Castel-Light Harbor had been no exception.

The yards had shut down stations eight, nine, ten, eleven, and twelve. Despite being the most recent in construction, twelve had been completely abandoned. It was rumored that the desertion of that particular station was due to some kind of insurance money. It now looked old and weathered. The tin roof and walls had begun to show signs of rust due to the lack of maintenance. Steel would have seen a better life expectancy, but Castel subbed out the construction to his father-in-law's construction company. Small town nepotism. Regina did her best to stay out of local politics unless it affected her. Most of the time, its impact came to zoning restrictions, which often threatened the roller rink. It would have been the prime location for a strip mall, but Grayson wouldn't budge. Thankfully, as long as Grayson kept the lease current, they couldn't touch it.

Regina walked over and shook the handle on the metal door. It was unlocked. She wasn't surprised, but she had expected it to be more difficult to gain access to this place. These buildings must have been some kind of safe haven for the homeless on really cold nights. That was if Bambi and her minions had not decimated the easy pickings that the homeless must have been. Regina pushed the door open slowly and cautiously stepped in. Veronica silently followed behind her. Regina stood at the entrance of the massive, empty building. It stretched to the length of a football field. The floor was wooden, with a slightly smoother kind of board than what the dock was made from. The small windows at the top of the building let in squares of grey light that dotted the floor along the length of the west wall.

Regina looked around knowing that she would be here again tonight, fighting for her life. She crossed her arms, realizing how cold she was in the open, dark, hollow hangar. She moistened her lips with her tongue as she looked around, still staring at nothing, hoping something would stand out at her or offer her an idea. But there was nothing. It was just a building. There was nothing inherently dangerous or scary about this place, but she couldn't help but fearing the very four walls that held up the structure. She looked over at Veronica, who was walking along the wall. Veronica found a large metal box with several large switches, and she flipped the one closest to the door on. Four rows of three bays of fluorescent lights flickered and hummed as they lit up the end of the building. The electrical system must have still been connected to some kind of main grid for the harbor or a generator was still functioning somehow. The harsh lighting did little to warm the place up. The humming disturbed several birds who were nesting on top of the light fixtures. They hopped from light to light before settling back down again, seeing the girls far below as no apparent threat to their safety.

"I guess this is the place," Regina said, just wanting to break the silence in the room. Her voice echoed slightly.

"Yeah," Veronica said, walking over to Regina. She sighed, able to see her breath even inside the room. It was cold.

"Hey, can I talk to you a second?" Veronica asked, like she had been putting every spare amount of thought into her next set of words. "It's about tonight."

Regina looked at her. By the tone alone, Regina knew she wasn't about to bail on her, but she was serious enough to be concerning. Veronica's eyes found their way to the floor. She hadn't turned away out of shame, she was just aware of her limits as a player and as a person.

"It's about my position." Veronica paused, the words clearly pained her. Even if only her pride.

"Tonight, I don't think I should pivot," she said.

In derby terms, the pivot was an important position. Not only did they serve as a blocker during the jam, but they could take the role of jammer if the opportunity presented itself. For their purposes, the pivot was also a potential assassin. Pivot was the backup if something were to happen to Regina.

"What do you mean? You're always my pivot!" Regina said, a little hurt and confused. "What if something happens to me? I need you there to take over and finish the job."

"I know," Veronica said, feeling the weight of every single word of it. "That's why I don't think I can do it. I'm not your pivot tonight." Veronica was genuinely sad that she had been bested, that there was someone better and more useful to Regina tonight. "You have somebody better. Lizzy is who you need. She's on fire, Regina. And if something does happen to you, she won't hesitate. She will be able to kill Bambi." Veronica paused briefly, but not long enough to give Regina a chance to argue. "I don't honestly know if I could do it. I'm still a kickass blocker—I've got your back, but you've seen her. She deserves this. She's the only one who can do it." If the time came, she was certain Lizzy could do what Veronica feared she couldn't. Kill. "I wouldn't tell you if I didn't think this was the right choice."

"But you're always my pivot. I like knowing you have my back," Regina said.

"I still have your back!" Veronica said earnestly. "And this way I can focus on it. I'll be able to just be a blocker without worrying 'what if I have to do this.'" Regina looked at her and nodded—no big fuss or fight. She understood. Regina had been watching Lizzy, too. Veronica was right. Lizzy was fueled by rage and heartbreak. Regina had seen it, and it had made her a stronger player. She was an animal, and when it came to fighting the vampires, an animal might be their best chance. Regina would have to put her faith in an untrusted and untested ally.

The girls stood around the building for a few more minutes until the cold got the better of them. They turned the light off as they left, leaving the room as black and empty as they had found it. They made their way back to the car, cranking the heat up to the highest setting until they hit the main road. Having finally knocked the chill from their bones, now they were simply left with the chill that remained in their souls. The night was coming whether they were ready for it or not. Regina dropped Veronica off at her apartment. She told her as she exited the car that she would be back in an hour. Regina instructed her to lock the doors behind her. She was sounding like Grayson, and it made her laugh. Regina watched her get in the door and close it behind her. For good measure, Regina quickly texted her to make sure everything was okay. She wouldn't make the same mistake she had made with Tabby. Her phone buzzed—an all clear. Regina dropped her phone into the cup holder where it rested on several old Starburst wrappers. She began to make her way back to her own home, alone for the first time in what seemed like ages.

She put her key in the doorknob and opened the door. As she stood in the doorway, she had the sensation that she was someplace unfamiliar. It felt empty. She felt almost like a stranger in her own home. Her roommate was nowhere to be found, as usual. She wondered if her roommate had even noticed that Regina hadn't been home in days. Probably not. That was one goodbye Regina felt no need to make.

She went to her room and closed the door behind her, dirty clothes spilling over the top of an unattended wicker laundry hamper. A mess was still strewn about on the floor. Photos of Grayson and several empty bottles of wine littered the bedroom. Regina sat at the end of the bed for a moment. *Where to start?* she thought. For the briefest of moments, she considered using the time she had left to clean up her bedroom. How embarrassing for her mother to come and collect her things if she did die, stumbling through this mess. It was just more encouragement to live. Someone had to clean up this mess, and it shouldn't be her mom. Regina grabbed her duffel bag from the top of the closet and began picking a few articles of clothing out of the top of a laundry basket sitting on the floor. Her arm hit the underside of an open drawer on her dresser, rattling it and causing a small bottle of lavender body spray to fall on the floor. She picked it up to put it back on the top of the dresser. Her eye caught a photo in the little ornate golden frame. It was her family. Mom, Dad, her two younger brothers. They were awkwardly posed on her grandmother's small loveseat. She sat up, grabbed the photo, and held it close to her chest. Looking at the picture of her family was the first time that she felt a real sense of worry that she might not make it out alive tonight. It hadn't concerned her to this point. She was fighting for what was right. She was a survivor, but it suddenly occurred to her what she might be leaving behind.

Regina reached in her pocket and pulled out her phone, scrolling through the recent contacts and calling her mother's number. She didn't know what she was going to say, she just wanted to hear her voice. She just wanted to have her say that everything was going to be okay.

The phone rang. It rang again. It rang again as tears began to well up in Regina's eyes. The phone continued ringing until the voicemail message started and rattled on until the beep sounded. It was almost too much to take—hearing her mother's voice telling her she was sorry that she missed her call, a generic message that everyone heard, but Regina chose to hear it like it was only meant for her.

Regina cleared her throat and put on a sweet, unassuming voice to casually leave her mom a message. "Just checking in. Love you," she said, quickly closing the phone shut and cutting off the message before she lost her composure. Regina set the photo down on the floor and crawled across the carpet, grabbing a notebook from the drawer next to her bedside table. She knew how she would spend her time. She set out to say goodbye. Regina had given the others a chance to do so, why should she not afford herself the luxury?

She wrote two letters—the first she folded and set off the side, and the second she reread before sealing it.

Mom, Dad, Jordan, and Graham,

I don't even know where to begin to tell you what is happening or, by the time you read this, what has already happened. I just really want you to know that I love you so, so much. And right now, writing this, I realize how much I really miss you guys. I wish you were here with me. I wish I were there with you and all of this had never happened. The less you know the safer you are. I got mixed up in something really bad. Something really dangerous. I was trying to help a friend, and things got out of hand. I don't know how to tell you anymore without putting you in danger, too. I know you will want to know what happened to me, and you deserve to know. But you can't. Just know that there are bad people in this world. I tried to stop them. You taught me to fight for what was right. Remember, Daddy? You taught me to never back down from a fight. I didn't. This time, I just didn't make it back. There is so much I want to tell you all. But none of it really matters. Just always remember that I love you. I can't even begin to thank you enough for everything you did for me. It hurts me so much to know that I was so far away from you guys. I don't have any regrets, though. Just know that. And when the time came, I was happy, and I was in love. To quote Great Grandma, "I was like a leaf in the autumn. I was most vibrant just before I fell."

Regina signed her name and jumped to the bottom of the page.

It was all she could do to bring herself to write to her parents. She had never considered how hard it would be to say her goodbyes. Regina wanted to tell them everything. She wanted to thank them for everything that they had ever done for her and list them in detail. She wanted to hug her mom one more time and give her dad a kiss on the cheek. She wanted to live. But if she didn't, most of all, she just wanted them to know that she loved them.

She finished the letter with a single sentence.

If Grayson makes it out, will you please see that he gets this letter?

She slid the folded letter with Grayson's name on it into the other folded letter, putting them both into an envelope and setting it on top of her dresser. Regina grabbed the bag off the bed. Passing through the vacant living area, she reached the door and stepped out into the cool, night air. Shutting the door behind her, she stopped on the sidewalk. She looked back at the little house she called home—the light blue wood paneling, the navy shutters, the little flower bed she never tended but always enjoyed looking at, and that ugly ceramic gnome. She wondered if she would ever see it again. She craned her head upwards as several geese called in the sky above her. She closed her eyes and put her hands together, bringing them to her chest.

Regina uttered a nearly silent prayer, asking the Lord to deliver her from her enemies, then she jumped back into her car and pulled out of the drive. She paused at the end, taking in the sight of her house one last time, then sped away to go back to Veronica's house.

Chapter Twenty-Four
Swords, Scars, and Sharpened Stakes

Veronica was already waiting on the porch, sitting on the steps as Regina pulled up to and slightly over the curb. A small calico cat circled around Veronica's feet, trying to nose its way into the day bag Veronica had placed next to her. The juvenile stray cat was looking for attention, having wandered around the neighborhood, seeking sympathy from every house she crossed. She whined and acted hungry until she had created a buffet of the neighborhood and she was waiting for Veronica to pony up her contribution to the all you can eat block party. Veronica stood up, snagging the bag and walking to the car, leaving the cat confused and slightly annoyed. It plopped down on the bottom step and started bathing its side, arm outstretched. Veronica opened the door to the backseat and threw her bag in, slamming the door behind her. She got into the passenger seat and buckled her seatbelt. The car lurched off of the curb as Regina pulled away and started back towards the rink where Grayson waited, putting together an arsenal of anti-vampire weapons.

The counter, which had once been used to hand out skates and hockey gear, was laid out with a line of items—all from the secret list Orbache had purchased. Orbache stood on the other side of the counter and watched as Grayson unloaded the plastic bag and set out the items. Orbache was fascinated as to what was to become of the random assortment of supplies. The razor blades, lighters, kerosene, electrical tape, boxes of matches, spray bottles, and spray paint—they seemed to be more the tools of a petty vandal than for use in some kind of master plan. But Orbache was also happy to not be whittling stakes anymore, his hands still recovering from all of the cramping. So, he waited patiently. He would enjoy the break.

Shortly after the girls left, Grayson had gone to the back, gathered all the brooms and mops he had in the building, and set them on the floor in front of Orbache. Orbache laughed to himself, thinking of Veronica trying to clean with the broken broom the night before. Orbache looked up at Grayson, hoping he wasn't suggesting that he should clean. Orbache did many things, but cleaning was not one of them. He rarely liked throwing around his wealth—normally he just took it for granted. It was practically second nature. But he was brought up in a house where he did not clean, and he certainly had no intent on acquiring that skill on what was potentially his last day on Earth.

"Start breaking those," Grayson instructed, motioning to the pile of cleaning supplies. "Sharpen them—we're going to need one for each of us, two for Regina and Veronica, about six inches long. Long enough to hit the heart."

There was something strangely familiar about it all. When he and Grayson had been younger, sometime before junior high, the two of them had built a fort in the forest behind Orbache's home on the back half of the estate. Grayson had practically lived with Orbache's family for the first year following the car accident that had claimed the life of his parents. Grayson had been placed under the custody of his uncle Marshall. Grayson's older sister, who had been eighteen at the time of the accident, had left. Grayson had resented her ever since, and hadn't laid eyes on her since his uncle's death three years prior. Throughout that first year, Grayson felt alone and disconnected. Orbache was the closest thing to real family he had to cling to. During one of their many days in the woods, they had sharpened the end of sticks, making swords in the event of an invasion. Back then, they were preparing for the threat of aliens. E.T. had scared the shit out of Orbache in particular. His giant eyes and spindly fingers still creeped him out to this day. In reality, the swords had mostly been used in battles between the two of them for dominance of the fort. One battle had resulted in a small scar that Orbache still sported on his shoulder.

The boys were dueling one winter afternoon. The snow had melted due to an unseasonably warm spell, which caused the large stone Orbache was balancing on to become slippery. He lost his footing, and Orbache had reached out and grabbed Grayson's sword in an attempt to stop his fall, but instead, he had overcorrected and came forward onto the sharpened end. The fall was forceful enough to puncture the skin and leave a nasty blue and yellow bruise that began surfacing almost immediately. They had decided to keep the entire incident a secret. Grayson feared Orbache's parents wouldn't let him come over anymore if they thought he had hurt Orbache—even by accident. Grayson was afraid he would be forced to spend his free hours working in the skating rink that his uncle owned.

Orbache had discarded his torn jacket and bloody shirt in the fort, wearing Grayson's jacket back to the house. They had cleaned his wound in the pool house so his parents and the house staff were none the wiser. It was an unceremonious blood brother ritual.

Sharpening the broken mop handle with a dull pocket knife reminded Orbache of that day. He shrugged his shoulder, brushing away the phantom pain. He also laughed a little. Orbache looked around at the rink, which remained mostly unchanged from how he remembered it as a kid. He couldn't help but be amused at how back then, Grayson had wanted nothing to do with this rink or his uncle. Of course, he knew most of that was probably a child's way of dealing with the loss of his parents. Rebellion, anger, frustration. Grief.

Grayson and his uncle had eventually become very close, and the rink became the closest thing Grayson ever had to a real home. Orbache knew that despite the time Grayson had stayed with him it wasn't his home. As lavish as it was, it was also cold and often sterile. Orbache's house was barely even a home to him.

Grayson's connection to the rink was the reason he had put the apartment in the back. It was financially beneficial, of course, but it was also Grayson's favorite place in the world. He had grown to love the rink—no one knew that more than Orbache. And when the day came that Grayson's uncle was too sick to keep it anymore, and the city was threatening a forced buyout for the land, Grayson offered to buy it from his uncle. He couldn't bear to see it be ripped down to make way for a Denny's or an authorized cell phone dealer. So with the money that Grayson had gotten from the sale of the unused engagement ring, Orbache offered to put up the rest of the money for the rink. Grayson promised him it was a loan, but Orbache had given it as a gift. Back then, he was just happy to be able to use his money for something other than weed and guitar parts.

Orbache stared down at the assortment of items on the counter and then looked up at Grayson, who was glancing at the items in deep thought, considering where to even begin.

"So, what is all this stuff for? How do you kill a vampire with duct tape?" Orbache joked.

"I'm not sure, but I figured it was good for everything else," Grayson responded, laughing.

He was really happy to have Orbache there with him. He was torn about bringing him into the situation, but nevertheless, he was glad he had him on his team.

"Vampires are not immortal. That is a good thing," Grayson stated as a known resolute fact. "They have fewer weaknesses than the rest of us, but fire is an equalizer. So is a stake to the heart or a beheading." Grayson was going over everything he thought he knew. "We have sunlight on our side, but I'm pretty sure they've been at this long enough to not be tricked into us stalling them until dawn. If it's the first thing I thought of, it's easily the first thing they learned to avoid," Grayson said, sounding like an expert on the subject and grateful for the wealth of information he had been able to acquire from the Internet. "So I thought we could outfit a couple of the girls on the sidelines with the kerosene in the spray bottles, and give the lighters to the players, and maybe we could burn them alive, so to speak. I'm sort of just grasping at straws. I thought we could use the razor blades to maybe get a couple of our players to give themselves a couple of nicks and distract the players with the scent of blood."

"Are those your best ideas?" Orbache asked, a little disappointed. "I saw *Blade II* like fourteen times, but maybe I missed the part where he was using razor blades, kerosene, and duct-tape."

"I'm making do, okay?" Grayson said, slightly defensive. "As long as Regina can stake Bambi, we won't even have to use any of this."

"Do you really think she can do it?" Orbache asked earnestly, propping himself up on the counter.

"Regina? Yeah, I think she can," Grayson replied with confidence. "I mean, I know she can do it. I know she can. It's the opportunity to get to Bambi—that's what I'm worried about. I don't think they are going to expect us to try and kill Bambi. I really don't. I think they just assume she has bought into this whole idea of winning the bout and saving Tabby." He paused. "At least I hope that's what they assume. It will make getting Regina in range to stab her a hell of a lot easier. If not, that's when we have a real fight on our hands."

Grayson sighed, acknowledging how fragile it all was.

Both Grayson and Orbache stood in silence for a moment, contemplating the plan as it was. Grayson broke the silence, focused again, saying, "Hey, start spray-painting those stakes black, will you?" He tossed Orbache a can of spray paint.

Grayson had something else that was practically eating him alive from the inside out in its nonstop attempt to escape his body and reveal itself. Somehow, he had managed to keep the topic at bay.

"Can I be really honest for a second?" Grayson said as Orbache shook the rattling can of spray paint. "I'm starting to get really anxious about tonight."

The marble settled back at the bottom of the can of spray paint. Orbache had been able to read this anxiety on his friend for most of the afternoon.

"Don't tell Regina, okay?" Grayson peddled back, almost trying to mentally erase the words from the air.

"I'm scared, too," Orbache said with a knowing nod.

He shook the can of spray paint once more, and it was never mentioned again. He covered his face with the end of his flannel shirt and began coating the wooden daggers in black paint.

Chapter Twenty-Five
The Pawn

Tabitha was starving. Her naturally thin frame and fast metabolism were currently to her detriment. The only sort of sustenance she had been given the entire time she had been in the vampire's possession was Gatorade. The mini-fridge in the corner was filled with nothing but bottles of Gatorade. Tabitha wasn't fully sure of the purpose it served, but she was fairly certain it was the only thing keeping her alive at this point. The vampires never touched it themselves, but it was the only item of food or drink in the entire building that she had seen. Granted, she hadn't been allowed to roam. As it were, she currently was propped up against the wall, chained to some kind of loading anchor.

In her lucid waking hours, her mind wandered. In those unconscious moments, her thoughts became nightmares that blurred the lines of what she would wake up to. Sanity was a far cry away, and she could feel herself losing touch with reality more and more with each episode of unconsciousness. She even began to question whether Regina and Veronica had actually come for her that night or if she had imagined it. Were they coming back to fight for her? The only reason she let it remain a real thought in her head was that she was still alive. They hadn't killed her. Regina *must* be coming back for her. She had to be. Since the death of the blonde girl, she had been alone in the dark, windowless room. Tabitha would've had no idea whether it was day or night if not for the visits from her nocturnal keepers.

Two of the vampires, Madeline and Victoria, would visit her. Always together, always just the two of them. Tabby assumed it was shortly after sunset each day. The first night she was there, they had beaten her mercilessly for the sport of it. They would lick the blood from her wounds as the skin swelled and split. She had overheard Bambi put a stop to that after Regina's visit. It wasn't done out of kindness, however—far from it, in fact. Bambi said she wanted her to look pretty the last time Regina would see her alive.

The pair had been annoyed that their fun was cut short. Tabitha was fairly certain she had heard them get scolded for calling out Bambi on her out-of-character obsession with the "brollerblader"– who she assumed was Grayson. First Regina, now Bambi. She just didn't get his appeal.

Tabitha had been grateful for the moments when she could preoccupy her time with less pressing thoughts than her own death—though she wasn't sure that she possessed the strength to survive much longer.

Tabitha wasn't even sure if she wanted to anymore. She wasn't sure what was real, and what was a dream. It was all a nightmare. All she knew for certain was that she wasn't a person anymore—she was a pawn.

Chapter Twenty-Six
Expendable Victims

Tabitha had time. Whether to her benefit or not, Regina had bought Tabitha time. If not for the risky wager on her life, Tabby would have certainly met her demise already. It wasn't the blood suckers' style to keep their victims alive for more than a few days. If you could even consider Tabitha *alive* at that point. Tabby was wearing her welcome thin, a house guest soon to be evicted. The chains that bound Tabitha to the wall bore messy remnants of dried, rust tinged blood from their previous occupant. Another expendable victim. He was on the menu. Tabitha knew she was destined to be the next course.

Less than a week before, this room had witnessed the last few strained gasps of air from Greg Harrington. In her solitary confinement she had begun to piece together that his disappearance was definitely the work of the vampires. This theory had been confirmed one evening as she overheard them cackling about his final hours. Victoria had even taken to wearing his jacket. Whether it was an ironic fashion statement, or a badge of honor, she was uncertain of. Tabby found herself looking around the room, thinking that these were the last things Greg had seen. Had he counted the rivets from corner to corner like she had? Did he notice there were missing screws on four panels? Had he traced circles in the dirt with his heels to pass the time? Tabitha found herself talking to his ghost. He never replied and never showed himself to her, but she was sure that he was listening. He knew what was coming for her. Greg wouldn't have let her go through this alone. He was a dummy, but deep down, he was a nice guy. The blonde girl was gone now. Her spirit somehow felt free. But Greg, he wouldn't leave her alone.

His experience had been different—a more typical captive for the blood-thirsty vixens. The vampires had sought her out, but he had gone right to them, willingly. Lured into a trap with the oldest trick in the book.

Greg had been seduced by blood sucking succubus.

Sexuality was a powerful weapon. Tabitha herself had known that strange kiss that had been blown to her shortly before her capture by one of the girls meant more than it seemed.

Her predicament had given her some mild insight into the group's dynamics she had hoped to use against them, but she had not been afforded the opportunity.

Aside from their brief chastising for questioning Bambi's motives, Tabitha had come to determine that Madeline and Victoria, the pair from the rink and her violent prison guards were second in command. Vicious and nasty to her, but strikingly gentle with each other. Tabitha had pieced together that they were in fact together. *A couple.*

These things were capable of feelings. Maybe even love. However, despite her pleas, it was a weakness Tabitha had not yet been able to exploit. With each moment passing she grew weaker and feared she would never get the chance.

Chapter Twenty-Seven

I Am the Warrior

When Regina and Veronica arrived back at the rink shortly after four-thirty, there was an air of unease that permeated the room from floor to ceiling. The stillness was foreboding. The silence was deafening. No one wanted to say it, but avoiding it was making the air almost too thick to breathe.

Regina walked along the counter surveying the wooden daggers, ready and waiting for their soldiers, eager for action and thirsty for blood. She picked one of the black pointed spears and held it in her hand. She gripped it firmly and took several steps away from the counter into the kitchen area. Regina stared at it, examining it as she held it under the overhead light. Unprovoked, she took the dagger and reared her arm back forcefully with a throaty shriek from the pit of her soul. Regina directed the dagger toward the shelf above the microwave and sent it deep into the side of a large metal can of artificial nacho cheese sauce. She removed it as quickly as she had sent it in, and wiped the yellow-gold sauce from the stake with a napkin that was sitting on the counter. The cheese oozed from the wound in the can. An innocent victim.

"Good to know it works," Regina said, explaining herself to the stunned stares of the others. She licked the remnants of the cheese off her fingers one by one.

However unorthodox, the tension had been broken.

"I was thinking about nachos for dinner," she said, smiling with a playful shrug. The others couldn't help but laugh.

"We don't have much of a choice now," Grayson said, perplexed but amused. "You know, those cans are like sixteen dollars a piece."

"$18.50, actually," Regina whipped back, per her unique brand of confident humor. Regina was laughing with them, but inside, she was torn up. Her hands were shaking, and she hoped they hadn't noticed. The tremors in her hands were threatening to encompass her whole body. She needed to get away.

"Going to go wash up," she said cooly, tossing the stake back on the counter and walking to the back. Regina made her way down the hall, feigning a chuckle and a bubbly appearance until she rounded the corner and was out of sight from the others.

She got into Grayson's bathroom and looked down at her hands—they were trembling uncontrollably.

When she had taken the wooden stake in her hand, she had been overcome with emotion. Regina had been devoured with a primal instinct to bury it deep within the target. It was like she had been trained to do so in a former life. The deeply buried urge was finally getting the chance to be brought to the surface. Regina tried to shake it out, rattling her hands down by her sides, but it was no use. She turned on the water as her hands still quaked. She let them rest under the stream of cool water until they finally began to relax and the tremors subsided. Regina washed her hands and dried them on the little pale green hand towel that hung by the sink. She exhaled deeply, releasing as much tension as she could from her body and her mind.

She looked up and stared at herself in the mirror. Regina reached down and took a small comb that was laying on the edge of the sink, using it to pick at her hair a little. She was trying to stall until she was sure her nerves were calm enough for her to fake an unbothered demeanor and safely rejoin the others without having to acknowledge her fear or show any weakness. Her eyes cut back to her reflection.

The person looking back at Regina as she thoughtlessly worked through her hair somehow looked older. This woman looked tired. This was a hardened version of the Regina who had carelessly looked in this mirror weeks before. She took some facial moisturizer from the medicine cabinet and massaged it into her skin. Aside from the dry winter air, the stress had caused her skin to look dry and pale.

The last thing Regina wanted was to look like one of them. Regina wanted to look alive. She wanted to be alive.

She opened the cabinet and rummaged under the counter, pulling out a small travel bag of makeup. It was full of small items and extras that she'd kept at Grayson's for the nights when she would stay over and then get ready for work the next day. It wasn't much, but it was something. She unzipped the bag and set a few items on the counter. She might not have felt confident, but she knew she could look it.

Regina began applying her foundation and a little bit of concealer underneath her eyes. The tinted base gave her skin a much needed warmth. A glow. She pulled out a palette and applied smokey eyeshadow with the slightest hint of silvery, shimmering purple. Her face lit up. She almost felt silly for putting on makeup, but she thought to herself, *Why shouldn't I feel pretty?* Why shouldn't she feel powerful, or at least give the appearance that she felt powerful?

Regina looked back into the mirror now and saw something different. Something different than anything she had seen before. They were just simple make-up techniques—practical applications on the normal woman, but on Regina today, it was war paint. She was a warrior. She licked her lips, swiped on a little lip gloss, and took one last look at herself before walking out the bathroom door and back down the hall. She walked with power, as if her life were a movie. She imagined this would be the scene where she walks in slow motion—the straightforward one-shot of her walking down the dark hall and emerging from the darkness into the light, walking with purpose, walking with power. Walking towards her destiny.

She rounded the corner and her eyes met Grayson's. He smiled at her, slightly caught off guard by her made-up appearance. She had never done her make-up before a bout, but she thought, *If not now, when?*

Grayson picked up the cheese-tested stake and tossed it to her. "When you gear up, keep your left wrist guard loose," he instructed. "It should slide under enough to conceal it while still giving you easy access to it." He had clearly been thinking about it.

Grayson walked around the corner of the kitchen counter and leaned in close to Regina. He quietly whispered in her ear as he passed her by to go lock the front door.

"By the way, you look really pretty." The blood rushed to her face. A little flattered, a little embarrassed. But completely enamored.

He went to the front and locked the deadbolt. While the girls had been gone, he and Orbache had affixed a piece of plywood to the hole where the glass had been broken. In reality, this was all just their own benefit. But he locked the door anyway.

This was all finally becoming real for them. They couldn't pretend it was a far off, hypothetical prospect. From the large windows on the front of the rink, they watched the day end and begin to melt away into night. They were silently aware of what sunset would bring. The only sound that interrupted the quiet wake for the day was the crunch of yellow corn tortilla chips dipped in lukewarm nacho cheese.

Regina hoped she would live through the night, if for no other reason than not wanting this to be her last meal. She had a lot of reasons for wanting to live, but this lackluster last dinner was now one of them.

Regina let out a sigh. The last sliver of light vanished behind the horizon. And with that, the sun had abandoned them. Before they knew it, it would be the witching hour. It would be time to fight. The rest of the team was set to meet them at the rink at ten. Until then, the door would stay locked. Until then, they could try and pretend tonight was just like any other Sunday night. Until then, they could pretend they weren't afraid.

Chapter Twenty-Eight
The Time Came

At 10 p.m. on the dot, an upbeat digital salsa tune rang out from the alarm Regina had set on her phone—completely unbefitting for the evening ahead. It was an alarm that was entirely unnecessary, reminding her of something that she couldn't have forgotten even if she had tried. The girls had arrived. Her small, but mighty team had come back. Early. They had all arrived well before the deadline. Perpetually optimistic or early to a funeral. Either way, they were here.

They had decided earlier in the day to wear their normal uniforms. Regina and Veronica, along with the girls, thought it would be fitting. In every aspect possible, they decided to try and treat this like any other bout. Wearing their colors. Supporting their team. Supporting each other.

Each girl donned her yellow tee, with the two black rings around the sleeves representing the stripes of the honey bee, their short, skin tight lycra black shorts, and high socks. Some of them wore yellow, some of them chose black. Regina always had to stand out a little. This was no exception. Her stockings were yellow with black stripes down the entire length of the leg. They were ripped, with runs littered all over them, but they were her lucky pair. Tonight, she could use all the luck she could get.

Grayson spoke to the girls as they were gathered around the tables. He updated them of the plan he'd been working on, explaining the ins and outs of what he knew about the vampires—their strengths, of which there were many, and their weaknesses, of which there were few. He and Orbache passed out the stakes as if they were celebrating a very gothic Christmas gift exchange. The girls stared at their homemade gifts, unsure whether to be grateful or afraid.

Regina watched him as he explained his plans to the group, going over all that he had learned that could be of any benefit. He seemed so strangely at home. He spoke about defeating them so confidently, so definite. For him, there didn't even seem to be a question that they could do it. The way he taught, it was like learning any other skill. Regina watched as he showed them how to use the momentum from a turn on the skates to help drive the stake into the flesh deep enough to damage. He had obviously put so much work into all of this, and Regina had no idea he had been this invested. Nor that he was good at it. It was the first time she had seen him in skates in ages. It was also the first time in a long time he seemed to be having fun.

"Everything I just told you guys is based on theory," Grayson qualified. "So we may have to change things up as we go. Just pray we've got something here that works or that we can work with. It will be about everyone staying observant. Stay on your toes—think fast, work smart, and I mean, play hard," he sort of shrugged and exhaled, realizing that there was nothing else he could tell them. He slid his own stake through the two belt loops in the back of his pants, pulling them up a little higher than he would normally have worn them and positioning his jacket so it would be sure to cover the weapon he was now concealing. He grabbed his backpack from the floor and lifted it up, pulling a bottle of caffeine pills from the front pocket and sitting them on one of the tables in the center of the group. "If you need these, they're here. No shame in needing a little pick me up," he added. "At this point we just try to see what will work."

"Maybe we should say a prayer?" Veronica suggested. It definitely couldn't hurt.

The group of girls was not overly religious, but tonight, no one put up a fight. A prayer actually seemed like a comforting idea to everyone. They all stood up awkwardly and with a hesitant, but instinctually collective mindset, they all reached out and began grabbing the hands of the girls next to them. Grayson, who was standing at the center with his green and grey backpack over his shoulders, took a slight step to the edge and held out his hand to Regina, motioning for her to take it. She placed her hand in his, and he clasped it. Regina in turn held out her hand to Veronica. The action repeated itself until they stood in a poorly formed circle, all holding hands. Orbache bowed his head, and the rest followed suit. The room was silent. No one had been elected to serve as the leader of this macabre prayer. Finally, Regina took it upon herself. She offered up a short and simple prayer, similar to the one that she had said earlier in the evening when she was standing in her yard and gazing up at the sun-drenched heavens.

"Lord, deliver us from our enemies," she said with sincerity and sadness. "Amen." Regina raised her head and opened her eyes, looking at her team.

"Amen," echoed throughout the group. It was a short prayer, no doubt—not the kind she had grown up hearing, but it was what needed to be said. A declaration for protection. It was the most they could ask for.

"There is no way to say all the things that should probably be said," Regina spoke, wanting to address the girls before the moment ended. "Thank you doesn't cut it. But it's all I have to offer." Regina could feel herself becoming flushed with emotion. "Thank you." She smiled at them and took one last look around the circle. Then her smile faded as quickly as it had arrived. "There's no more time for stalling though. It's time. Let's play a good game," Regina championed. "We can beat them. We can do this. I know you can. I know *we* can. We can win." She took a moment and quickly corrected herself, "We *will* win."

Regina had always seen those rallying cries in the movies. Those speeches that instilled confidence. She could barely muster the confidence of a line cook at Waffle House rallying for the 3 a.m. rush, but she had given it everything she could.

Chapter Twenty-Nine

Lurking in the Shadows

The town had a silver luster under the mist-muted moon as the caravan of cars headed towards the docks. Regina glanced back several times in her rearview mirror just to make sure she still saw the line of headlights trailing her. The headlights sparkled and shined in the cold mist, drifting from the overcast sky above. A fog would settle in soon. With each momentary relief of seeing she wasn't alone, she refocused on the road. The windshield was becoming littered with moisture, her windshield wipers clicking on and slapping the condensation from her view. For Regina, a lot of things were much more clear. She looked over to her right. Sitting next to her in the passenger seat was Grayson. He'd been staring straight forward, intent, thoughtful. His knee bounced nervously. Occasionally, he would tap his fingers on his leg like it was the keys of a piano. No melody, just some song in his own head. Veronica ran her fingers through her hair as she pulled it into two loose pigtails at either side of her head. The movement caught Regina's eye. Veronica twirled the end of one of the pigtails in around her fingers, and it was hard to know if it was continued styling or a response to the stress.

Orbache unbuckled his seatbelt unannounced, and reached up in between the seats, and clicked on the radio.

"It's not doing any of us good to sit here in silence," he said, as if the quiet had been a personal attack on his sanity. He slouched back into the seat and fastened the seatbelt back with a loud click. "Safety first and all," he added with good natured sarcasm that fell on deaf ears.

The Top 40 station ended the silence of worry and fear, but each of them was still deep in thought. The playlist of the evening was forgotten quickly as each song was played. None of them could have recalled a single song that they heard, and although Orbache did his best to provide some modest entertainment by drumming loudly along with the radio on the back of Grayson's seat, it was as absentminded as everything else that evening. Until they got to the warehouse, they were just going through the motions, running on borrowed time.

Few cars passed by them at this hour. Most people were in their homes asleep or preparing for work the next morning. The occasional sight of other nocturnal travelers on the street basically vanished as they drove deeper into the outskirts of town toward the shipping district.

Regina wondered about the people in those other cars. Where were they going? Who they were going home to see? She envied them. Not just that they got to go home tonight. Regina envied them mostly because they had the privilege of being unaware of the dangers that were hidden in the world. Like a child learning the hard way of the heat of a stove, she had touched the white-hot reality of the dangers in the darkness and she would never forget it—no matter how hard she tried. Regina knew that no matter what happened tonight, she would never be able to go back to the life she had before. A life before vampires.

Regina's car led the strangest of funeral processions. She wove them back down the gravel road to Building 12. Her heart sank, and a knot twisted itself in her stomach as she saw an ominous glow in the dark when they approached. The lights in the warehouse were on. They glowed from the tiny windows at the top of the building. The vampires were already there. They were waiting for her. She knew they would be. Regina wasn't surprised, but despite her best efforts to prepare herself, she had secretly hoped they would not show up, that maybe they left town during the night, and she would walk in to find Tabby had been left in their haste. Any lingering hope of that forfeit was now dead. She hit the brakes, and the car crawled to a stop. She slipped the gear shift into park, clicked the notch, and unbuckled herself, losing one last sense of security. She took a deep breath and stepped out of the car. The moist night air hit her like a barrage of icy needles stinging her face and hands. She winced at the cold as the other two cars carrying the rest of the team pulled in beside her. The passengers in Regina's caravan of death slowly exited and awkwardly stood around, trying to brace themselves against the chill in the air that none of them could shake.

They did their best to stand at attention—her makeshift army. They were waiting for Regina to give them their orders. Shifting their weight from side to side, adjusting clothing, no one was certain what came next. Regina looked over, realizing that the passengers of her own car had not exited. Veronica finally got out of the car and walked over, standing next to Regina. Regina could still feel the heat from the car as it clung to Veronica's sweater. Orbache was not far behind, though he only walked a few steps and leaned himself against the car, stealing the warmth on the hood of the car from the recently shut off engine. Grayson was still in the car. Alone. He sat silently. His nerves were haywire—he tingled with energy. He took a shaky, deep breath and pulled his jacket tight around him, finally stepping out of the car, much to Regina's relief.

Even though he had ridden there with her, he still got out of the car. He came through. He showed up for her. He believed in her. She could believe in herself, too. It was a much needed boost of confidence.

Treat it like any other game, she kept repeating in her mind. She was trying to believe that, even though it most certainly was not. Regina gave a nod to the team and rallied her confidence. It was time to go.

The group began heading toward the building, making their way through the shoddy fence. They were within twenty five yards of the warehouse. Regina was thankful that the lights lining the dock had come on. She assumed they were all on one switch or grid. She couldn't imagine the vampires had thought to politely light the half-mile walk from where they parked to the warehouse. With the building in sight, Grayson jogged up to Regina from his spot where he had been bringing up the rear.

"Hey, hold up. Can I talk to you for a second?" Grayson asked, grabbing her arm. It caught her off guard. His tone was serious, but there was something else in it she couldn't place. Nerves? Excitement? She stopped dead in her tracks and turned to him. His face was shadowy. She could barely make out his features as they stood in the gap of the light poles. She thought she could see his half-smile.

"Guys, wait for me at the door," she called to the rest of the team as they began to walk past her. "I'll be there in a second. We go in together."

The group kept walking. Veronica looked back, and Regina gave her a little nod that she would be okay. The two of them were left alone in the dark.

The sound of the waves lapping at the edge of the dock was rhythmic and haunting. The cold caused the noise to travel. It was louder than Regina had remembered it being during the day. Grayson slid the backpack from his shoulders and it hit the ground beside him. Several items went spilling out of the front pocket. The zipper was broken, but Grayson refused to get a new backpack or let Regina repair it. It was something familiar and comforting. Something mundane.

Regina smiled with a half laugh and went to bend down to pick the glow sticks and batteries up off the ground, but Grayson grabbed her hand and held her back. He guided her back up to a standing position and knelt down on one knee in front of her. At first, Regina just thought he was preparing to pick up the casualties of the backpack spill or tie his shoe, but then as the moon shifted out from under the cloud cover, she could see his face looking up at her, her hand still well eclipsed within his. She didn't really have time to process what she was seeing before he started speaking.

"Regina," he said gently, but with purpose. "I should've done this three years ago, and I chickened out." He nodded, trying to let her know that he was aware of his faults. He was aware that this had taken years longer than it should. He was trying to signal that he was ready—he was in it for the long haul. His voice was shaking with nerves as he reached into his jacket's breast pocket. He pulled out a small ring box. "Regina—"

He was immediately interrupted. Regina took her hand from his and put it on his shoulder. She tried to make him stand up, grabbing at the fabric of his jacket.

"Grayson, don't do this," she pleaded. "Please get up." Regina heard the words coming out of her mouth and hated herself for saying them, but she had no control to stop them. "Grayson, we're good now," she said frantically, trying to explain herself. "But look at what it took to get us here. Grayson, please." She was furious with herself. Why was she doing this? She wanted to marry him. Why was she sabotaging his attempt to marry her? Again?

"Grayson, we're broken," she said, honestly. Word vomit spilled out, with no filter and nowhere else to go.

Grayson was not swayed this time. Not this time. Not like he had been three years ago. Not like when he'd hung on to the last ring so long, he'd forgotten he had it. This time, Grayson would propose to her.

Regina would be his wife.

Grayson had made that decision laying next to her in bed the night prior. He had snuck out the next morning to get the ring. He had sent messages to eighteen jewelry stores and two pawn shops in the middle of the night and was finally able to persuade the proprietor of a family-owned jewelry shop three towns over to open up early on a Sunday with the promise of a substantial purchase. Grayson had taken the five-thousand dollars Orbache had left for him to escape and decided to use it for the complete opposite. He wanted to use it to stay. To settle down.

Despite the dampness from the dock that was now seeping through the knee of his jeans, he was determined to stay there until she answered him. Until she said the words that filled him with excitement. Indescribable nerves and immeasurable happiness. He was not going to back down this time. Grayson looked over at the fallen items from his pack.

"You're right, Regina," he said, a puff of breath visible on the air. "We *are* broken."

Regina was stunned and a little hurt that he agreed with her.

He reached down and picked up one of the glowsticks from the ground.

"But Regina, I think that's a good thing," Grayson continued. Regina's face could not have been more confused if Grayson had told her he too was a vampire. "We're just like this glow stick, Regina." He was being sincere and sweet and not making any sense with his unpolished illustration. "We had to be broken and shaken up before we could really shine," he said as he snapped the glow stick and shook it, making the liquid inside the plastic tube casing radiate with a bright green glow. He looked up at her, lit in the green neon light.

Her soft features were highlighted ever so gently, the glow cascading across her skin for Grayson's own personal visage of a human aurora borealis. Her eyes twinkled and sparkled as the cold air and her heightened emotions gave them a glassy and mesmerizing quality so clear, he was certain he could see her very soul. She radiated beauty and strength. Comfort. Home.

Regina looked down and saw his dumb, innocent face, so genuinely in love with her. Meaning every word of his corny gesture.

Regina put her hands up over her mouth, trying to hide the overwhelming grin that threatened to consume her entire face and stretched her cheeks so much, it caused her eyes to squint. She busted out into laughter. "That was the dumbest thing you've ever said," she cackled. She stopped laughing, not wanting to hurt his feelings. She dropped her hands to her chest, clasping them together. "And also one of the sweetest things I've ever heard in my life."

Grayson smiled at her.

"Regina, will you marry me?" he asked without hesitating a moment longer. It was a question he had wanted to ask her so many times. He wanted her forever. However long forever may have been at that point, he wanted to spend it with her.

She smiled at him and prepared to answer, but their tender moment had caused them to let down their guard. Grayson's proposal had unfortunately been the perfect diversion. They had not seen the shadowy creatures approaching in silence. During the loving moment, they had been consumed within themselves, oblivious to the dangers still lurking in the world. The pair had not been paying attention to the darkness surrounding them. Madeline, Victoria, and two other butchers from the Mother Suckers emerged from the umbrage, grabbing Grayson from behind and yanking him backward to his feet with a surprising amount of force. Regina screamed. She was startled by the sudden movement then horrified when she realized what was happening. She was trying to wrap her brain around what was going on, every instinct rushing back after their momentary recess.

Grayson was trying to fight back and get free, but as much as it hurt his pride, the women were easily overpowering him. He could not escape their grip. He wildly flung his lower body like a toddler being drug away from the playground, not ready to leave. Grayson wasn't ready to leave.

"Let him go!" Regina yelled angrily, already reaching for the dagger hidden in her wrist guard. She was willing to throw away the entire plan in that moment to save Grayson.

"You'll see him again," Madeline cackled at her. "Maybe."

"Yeah, but right now he has a special seat waiting for him in the winners circle," Victoria chimed in. "That's where we keep our prizes."

The three other girls began dragging him away toward the warehouse. Grayson was still kicking, trying to fight them off to no avail.

"I said let him go!" Regina said, nearly lunging at Madeline.

"Nuh-uh." The stocky and snotty woman stuck up a single finger in Regina's face. "Not so fast, bumblebee. You know the deal. You get him back if you win," she said, flatly cordial.

Regina wanted nothing more than to rip that finger off her damned undead hand.

Madeline turned from Regina and started walking away, following the girls dragging Grayson, who was now trying to dig the heels of his boots into the dirt to slow his captors. Regina could do little more than watch. They were taking him away from her.

Regina started running after them. "Grayson! Grayson! My answer is yes!" she said, screaming into the night air. "I am going to get you back!" she cried out to him again. "I am going to get you back!"

She was too angry to cry. Too scared to even really think. She was moving and functioning now on pure adrenaline. She was on aggressive autopilot.

Regina turned back around and grabbed Grayson's backpack from off the ground. She gently picked up her engagement ring that had fallen to the ground in the attack. This wasn't how she ever imagined it. It wasn't how she dreamed of this moment as a child. She brushed away the sand from the setting and slipped it on her finger with no time to even admire it. It was a beautiful ring. The rock caught the lights from overhead and sparkled. Regina slung the backpack onto her shoulder and bolted towards the rest of the team who had been waiting for her at the large roll-up warehouse door. She nearly ran right into them, not expecting to have met them in the middle. They were coming towards her, having heard all the commotion, her calvary. She slowed, but instead of stopping, she just kept forcefully walking right through them. Barely noticing their questions and concerned remarks of what was going on.

"What happened?" Orbache asked, repeatedly, his impatience was unmistakable. "Where's Grayson?"

"They took him," Regina said, still walking quickly towards the door. She feared if she slowed her momentum, she might fall apart.

Orbache ran, catching up to her. The rest of the team doubled back around, following Regina to the front of the warehouse.

"What do you mean they took him?" Orbache asked angrily.

"They took him," Regina answered without missing a step. A woman on a mission. "He's a prize—that's all he is to them."

Orbache was in disbelief. At the situation. At her calm over it. "Regina," he responded, nearly stumbling as he tried to wrap his head around what she had just divulged.

"We'll get him back when we win." She paused abruptly and took a single step in reverse, turning and facing Orbache. He almost ran into her, not expecting her to stop short. Their faces were barely six inches apart.

"And we *will* win," she summoned the words from the pit of her soul through gritted teeth.

Orbache nodded. He wanted to believe. He had no choice but to believe her. Regina turned back around and stomped forward, marching towards the metal door. Her pace began slowing only as her feet touched the concrete pad of the loading area.

The door stood in front of her. Her team behind her. She took a deep breath and wrapped her hands around the cold metal handle, swinging open the door. Regina was prepared to play the roller derby bout of her life.

Chapter Thirty
The Plight of the Captives

The door caught no resistance and slammed against the wall as she forcefully opened it. The building was busy with Edgar Allan Poe's fan club rolling around the floor. The loud noise caused them to stop and turn, staring at her as Regina walked into the building. The rest of her team funnelled in the door and spread out behind her. Bambi rolled up, wind whipping her midnight hair as she slid to a stop.

"Your team is looking a little sparse," Bambi mocked. "Did they chicken out, Regina?" She smiled, her fangs ever evident. Regina wondered whether she were capable of concealing them, or had she just missed them before? She could see them now, and they were smiling at her.

Regina smiled back. "Just the opposite, in fact." The two women bantered like the worst of old friends. "I told the rest of the girls they could take the night off." Regina chuckled. "They've seen me beat down skinny pale bitches before," she guffawed. "You know, I'd rather them get a good night's sleep than sit and watch a rerun."

"Cute," Bambi said, unamused.

Regina had struck a nerve. She knew it. She was in her head. She might not have been nervous, but Regina was certain that she was occupying space in Bambi's thoughts.

Because Regina was more of a threat than Bambi wanted to admit. That's why Bambi had put into place a plan B.

She had instructed her team, if the bout turned outside their favor, they would simply kill them all. Of course, even if the bout *did* go their way they were going to kill them all. The Bloody Mother Suckers did not lose. Of course, the Bloody Mother Suckers had also never been challenged by humans. Bambi was unaware that Regina and the Hunny Bees had actually planned ahead and were prepared for just such a showdown.

"You can lace up over there." Bambi gestured across the floor. "It should give you a nice view of the winner's circle. I wanted you to at least get to see what it looks like." Bambi flipped her hair, like she'd studied at the school of shrew from every late 80s romcom. "Even if it's just from a distance," Bambi said as she wheeled to the side, giving Regina full view of a pyramid shaped stage constructed of old wooden shipping pallets, stacked layer upon layer and creating a rickety staircase to the top platform. At the top, Grayson was tied to a makeshift wooden chair. If it weren't for his restraints, he would've looked like a king perched on his cobbled throne to oversee the bloodbath below. Next to him, tied like a witch at the stake was

Tabitha. She was strapped to some sort of metal bar. It wasn't a part of the building's structural support. They had placed it there for effect. Several large glass beer steins rested by her feet—those did not seem to be there only for show. They definitely looked practical.

"Is there going to be beer afterward?" Orbache whispered, barely loud enough to hear and almost to himself, turning to Veronica as she also noticed the mugs.

Bambi was unamused by the guy she vaguely recognized from the bar. A blood refinery and nothing more, she'd drain him right now and not think twice about. She smiled at him.

"No, you dimwit. When we win, we're going to slit your friend's throat and toast to our success with her blood," Bambi answered. She turned and took a few strides away from them before craning her head back. "Twenty minutes," she called. "I'd suit up if I were you." She rejoined her team by the rails of the rink.

Regina fumed as they headed to their side of the rink to finish getting dressed. They had Tabby strung up like some kind of living scarecrow and planned on tapping her like a keg and drinking the life from her. It made her even more angry to see that they had clearly dressed Tabby for the occasion. Showy. She was draped in what looked to be some kind of cheap flowy toga or old wedding gown. It was white. It would show the blood best when they drained her right in front of Regina. She knew that was for her. But the way Grayson was positioned—that was done for Bambi. As the queen, she intended to take her king.

Regina was queen bee, and she had no plans on losing the title. She sat down on a long wooden bench and unzipped her bag. Next to her skates were the remainder of her wooden stakes. She was ready for them now. She was ready to kill.

The old warehouse building looked completely different than how it had earlier in the day. Regina had to hand it to the vampires—they had clearly perfected these pop-up style rinks. If she didn't hate them so much, Regina might have taken time to pick their brains about their set up process. Travel leagues would kill for space options like this. I guess that is one of the benefits of years of trial and error. Perhaps decades. Maybe even since the sport's initial rise to fame in the seventies. Who knew? Maybe vampires had invented roller derby, and the humans happened to find out about it and claim it as their own. Maybe it was their sport first. If that was the case, it must have really annoyed Bambi that Regina was so good at something their kind had created.

As she looked around, it was a full layout. Set up in the now repurposed warehouse, there were particle board half walls, chairs, and taped-off rink lines that seemed to the naked eye to be regulation quality. It was to a tee, a well put together rink. Regina couldn't imagine what their lives must be like—nomadic, on the run. Hiding in the shadows.

From over her shoulder, she heard the sound of laughter, almost a giggle. It was lighthearted and warm. Regina turned to see what could have been so amusing to her team in a time like this. She could have used a little levity herself. But the joyous and infectious laughter wasn't coming from *her* team. It was three of the other girls. Vampires. They smiled and laughed; the taller girl rested her hand on one of the others' shoulder and gave it a gentle, encouraging squeeze. For the briefest of moments, they seemed so purely human that it threatened to throw Regina off her game. For the first time, she wondered what Bambi must have been like before she was a vampire, before she had become so blood-thirsty and cold.

Were there vampires who retained a heart? Who kept a soul? Were all vampires destined to become an empty shell of their human selves, death-craving and cruel, or were they capable of more? Regina actually felt sorry for Bambi in the most fleeting of thoughts. Bambi probably wasn't even her real name. Hopefully it wasn't her real name. *But then again,* she thought, *who'd voluntarily choose that as a name?* Regina laughed to herself as she carried on the conversation in her head while lacing up her skates. It was actually common practice for her to create these full narratives for her opponents. Though never had a rivalry been this serious.

That girl had probably had a family. The thought landed uncomfortably in the pit of her stomach. Before she was a vampire, she had probably been loved—maybe she even loved somebody once. Regina glanced over at Grayson, tied to the chair atop his temple in the corner behind the black wooden painted half wall. Maybe Bambi had been in love with a man who had looked like Grayson. Maybe he even had Grayson's eyes. Did they share the same sweet and relaxed demeanor? Maybe he had spoken softly to her. Encouraged her with a stern and deep-rooted purpose. Regina guessed he loved her back. Perhaps that's what she saw in him—maybe Grayson offered some connection to her lost humanity. Regina wondered if maybe that's why she was so fascinated by him. Regina began to genuinely feel something for her. She felt sorry for her. But Regina quickly shook it off. She refused to humanize any further the monster that Bambi was now. Bambi had lost her man who may have looked like Grayson. That was something they shared. Regina knew what it felt like to have lost him. But Regina wasn't going to lose him again. Bambi had maybe lost her own Grayson, but she was not going to get Regina's.

Regina looked down at the ring on her finger and smiled. She was going to win this or kill Bambi trying, one way or the other, Bambi was not getting her teeth or any other part of her body near Grayson. If Bambi was hurting over losing someone like Grayson, well Regina was damn sure she would help put her out of her misery. Permanently.

Bambi's motive, however, had been much less storybook. Regina had challenged her, in a way that Bambi had not been challenged in ages. It was thrilling. But it had caused ripples of dissension among Bambi's followers. Humans were food. Humans were for frivolity. Humans were not equals. Grayson had become a prize out of calculated necessity.

Bambi had planned on draining him the night she stopped him on the sidewalk, but his blood alcohol level had clearly been too high, and it made his blood too thin to clot for repeated feedings. He was a waste of a body for everything but his body. They'd gone back out and found the blonde girl sulking in the alley, and she'd sufficed. Grayson's survival made for an interesting addition to her showcase of terrors. Bambi wanted to watch Regina crumble as she would turn him and then force Regina to watch him feed for the first time on Tabitha. It was all a bit dramatic, but Bambi did have a flair for showmanship.

Grayson sat in the chair, outwardly calm despite his dire predicament. He was trying to remain cool—he knew that for any of this to work, for him to survive, he had to keep his wits about him. In the last few days, he had become a different person, a better version of himself. He had grown up. He had found a purpose. Grayson hadn't told Regina, so as not to add more to her plate already full of worry, but he had planned for becoming a captive. In the back of his mind, he knew that he would not be allowed to just stand and cheer for Regina. They had made it clear he was a prize. Hidden within the cuffs of his jacket were razorblades. He'd pulled the stitches from the fold at his wrists and slid them in. They were invisible. Grayson had duct taped one side to hopefully give himself a better grip and mitigate the risk of slicing his skin open. His blood would surely draw attention to the escape plan. He began working them loose with his fingers and silently positioned it between his finger and his thumb, patiently sawing and nicking away the ropes that bound his hands. Despite his best efforts, the razor blade dug in and left small cuts on his fingers and the skin of his arm as he blindly scratched at the rope. He did his best not to flinch. They were mostly just uncomfortable, and so far, nothing deep enough as to draw blood to the surface. Grayson ignored the discomfort and kept trying to free himself. Once his hands were unbound, he could untie the ropes at his legs and waist. It was the only way he could possibly be of some real help. But he had to get loose first.

Thankfully, the two women who were standing guard at the bottom of the pile had gone over and joined the rest of the team. Grayson knew with their departure that the match must be starting soon. He was grateful for the reduced security on him, but he was beginning to worry about the time crunch. He was now alone on the stack with Tabby. They were easily fifteen or sixteen feet above the ground. Grayson thought he could jump down safely, but there was no way he could do it with Tabby over his shoulder. He would have to try and climb down the pallets with her. Grayson had been trying to get her attention, speaking to her, but if she was conscious, she could not hear him. He was honestly just hoping she was still alive. He watched her for a few moments to see if she was still breathing—if she was, it was shallow. Deathly shallow breaths. She didn't have much time left. Whether the vampires drained her or not, she would not make it much longer than the night.

"Tabitha," he whispered loudly, watching to make sure he could not be heard. "If you can hear me, I'm going to get us out of here. We are all going to get out of here," Grayson promised. "Tabby, can you hear me?"

Tabitha stirred for the first time since she had been roughly thrown on the metal rod earlier. She rocked her head slightly forward. Grayson wasn't sure whether it was an acknowledgment or an involuntary action, but he chose to believe it was a nod—he chose to believe it was an acknowledgment. She had heard him. *Keep hope alive,* he thought. He kept working away at the ropes that bound him as the girls all made their way onto the rink.

Chapter Thirty-One
Meant to be Broken

The Hunny Bees skated to the center of the taped off rink as Bambi and the Bloody Mother Suckers did a lap around the perimeter of the rink. Bambi led, waving a large black flag, displaying the team's insignia on it. An abstract bat, outlined in wisps of white, silver, and red popping against the black fabric of the cloth flag, it reminded Regina of a more sinister version of the bat she had seen on bottles behind the bar after countless shows, while making small talk with bartenders and waiting for Grayson and the band to load their gear into the van so they could go home. There was no sitting and waiting to go home tonight. Regina reached up and touched the little felt bumblebee on her helmet. The cute bee was no match for Bambi's evil bat. She only hoped she herself would fare better.

Bambi tossed the flag pole to the side. It clanged against the floor and rolled under several chairs on the edge of the building. Regina slipped on the cloth cap with the star over her helmet. She looked over and smiled sadly at Veronica, who was adjusting the striped cap on Lizzy's helmet. Lizzy now donned the strip that signified her newly-minted status as pivot.

"Regina, I can do this, don't worry," Lizzy said, truly meaning every word of it. "I won't let you down."

"I know you won't," Regina replied, patting her head encouragingly.

Lizzy was ready. The black war paint smeared under her eyes gave her tired face a hollow and skeletal appearance. Regina had brought her very own ghost to the undead battle royale. *Fire with fire,* she thought. Lizzy touched the little star pendant around her neck for luck. Lizzy had brought a ghost with her, too.

Bambi slowed herself to a rolling stop on a straight white line that crossed the width of the track. ""If you would join me, Regina," Bambi beckoned, "And we'll get this started." She crouched down into an adjusted runner's stance.

It was now or never. Regina took one last quick glance over her team as they stood behind her. Ready to play. She then glanced over at the prizes. Tabby forcibly stood at attention, a literal death totem, and Grayson sat so calm, so oddly calm. Regina blew him a kiss and wiggled her fingers hoping he could see the twinkle of the ring on her finger. He smiled at her and nodded. Regina could wait no longer. She skated over next to Bambi and crouched down. Bambi turned and looked at her, smiling a creepy, toothy grin and showing off her two protruding fangs.

"I'm going to kill you," Bambi smiled before pushing her mouth guard into place.

Regina smiled back. "Not if I kill you first."

The remainders of both teams were lining up a mere twenty feet in front of their jammers. For what it was worth, so far this was very similar to most derby bouts. Regina and Bambi would have to fight to close that twenty foot gap. They would have to get through the girls and then around again. Their goal was to lap them. They would receive points for every blocker they passed after the initial breakthrough lap. It seemed so simple—just skate around them really fast, how hard could it be? Regina's heart felt like it was about to burst right out of her chest. She could hear it in her ears, a pounding and rapid *thump thump thump*. It was loud enough that she was sure Bambi could hear it as she cut her eyes over at Regina. Regina ignored the look and closed her eyes, trying to calm herself. Her eyes opened only as the whistle blew and Bambi's padded elbow made direct contact with her face. It caught her so off guard, she stumbled and fell to the ground as the other skaters raced ahead of her.

Regina quickly stood up, blood running from her newly busted lip. She stood waiting for a penalty to be called for the grossly illegal hit. She then quickly realized the foolishness of her assumption—there would be no penalties called. There would be no rules followed. This would not be a fair game. It wasn't her style, but Regina could play that way, too.

She took her forearm and ran her mouth along the length of it, leaving a streak of bright red blood across her skin. She flicked and splattered several drops on the ground before taking off, already behind. Any hopes of a head start were DOA. The other girls were already closing in on her. They had almost made a full lap, and she was just standing still. The clock was ticking—she had no time to waste. 120 seconds to save the world. Regina put so much power into the race, towards catching up to Bambi, that she could feel the muscles in her thighs tensing and shredding beneath her stockings. Her flesh burned from the inside, but she didn't care. She caught the eyeline of Lizzy and Veronica, who hit two of the Mother Suckers hard with their shoulders, clearing a path for Regina to easily come up the center. Regina pushed forward and made her way up the middle of the girls, now trailing only a few feet behind Bambi, who was a regrettably agile skater.

Bambi whipped around, trying to leave Regina behind her as she hit the turn. It was an ineffective move. Soon, both girls began making real headway from the rest of the team. Scoring was becoming a closer and closer tangible possibility. Grasping the first point was within both their reaches.

The team was now behind them to the point where they were in close proximity to lapping the blockers. That is where the scoring would begin, the moment they began weaving through the team again. Bambi was fast, and Regina was honestly having a hard time keeping up with her, but she pushed forward, skating nearly shoulder to shoulder with her. With pure grit force, she reached her and was able to maintain her speed. Regina was keeping up. They each began trying to forcefully nudge the other off the track. Blood was running down Regina's face from her lip. Regina could feel it mixing with sweat and scattering across her skin. She tried sucking her lip into her mouth to catch the blood, but that made little difference thanks to her mouth guard.

Out of the corner of her eye, she could see Bambi looking at her bloody misfortune and smiling. It was at that moment, Regina decided to play by their rules: no rules at all.

She had thrown the first punch, and it was time for Regina to fight back. Retaliation. She took her hand and ripped her mouthguard from in between her teeth, spitting the blood that she was collecting in her mouth into Bambi's face and catching her completely by surprise, creating a state of bewilderment for the vampire vixen. The stunt was temporarily disorienting enough for Regina to pull ahead of Bambi. Bambi had to slow enough to wipe the blood from her face, giving Regina her first real advantage.

"That's the only taste of my blood you're gonna get, bitch," Regina muttered under her breath. "I can pull a cheap shot too."

Veronica turned and saw Regina coming up the rear of the pack. "Clear a hole!" she screamed.

The vampires saw what had happened and quickly tried to compensate for their temporarily handicapped leader, but the Hunny Bees were having none of it. Clotheslining two of them, tripping another, and one simply just fell out of confusion after she stumbled over the speed bump of her wiped out team member.

Bloody Mary took another vampire out when she forcefully rammed her shoulder into her. It was a legal, although painful attack. Mary had actually dislocated her own shoulder in the process, but being no stranger to a little rough play, she whipped her torso, sending her arm flinging wildly like a rag doll and popping it back into the socket, no worse for wear.

Lizzy looked back—Victoria was right behind her. Bambi's right hand woman was the last thing blocking Regina's path straight up the line. Lizzy turned to Abby, who was next to her and trying to fight off Tessa, a scrawny, but vicious Mother Sucker. She would be of no help. Lizzy was on her own, and she had a wild idea.

This is why Regina had given her this position. She could do what Veronica wouldn't, couldn't. Lizzy was certain Veronica would never do this. Lizzy had once been a decent gymnast. She had torn her anterior cruciate ligament training for a competition in her junior year of college. She had met her husband in rehab, and once she had gotten pregnant, she never went back to the sport for more than stretches and exercise. But she never lost her passion for it. Lizzy was pretty confident she had enough muscle memory left to pull off one last stunt.

Lizzy skated ahead of the girls, keeping an empty distance of only a few feet. It was all she needed. She pulled ahead and stopped abruptly, turning around to face the oncoming team and the brick house that was Victoria. Lizzy was moving slowly backward, leaning back on her left leg. She kicked her right leg up into the air, and the four wheels of her skate met squarely center with Victoria's unsuspecting face. A guttural, pained groan exited Victoria, and black blood drenched face. The maneuver had been none too comfortable for Lizzy either. She felt it in her knee with the connection of the skull and the momentum of her opponent's body. The risky move sent the two of them forcefully down, tangled, crashing, meeting with the hard wooden floor.

Victoria's face hit the slatted lumber hard. She skidded, her knee pads doing little to slow the propulsion of the fall. Her body scraped across the floor, and in the midst of the skid, a foot-long piece of the floor the was fractured away from the floorboard splintered between the flesh of her face and her skull. She stood up and screamed. The long broken sliver of wood had gone through her cheek and eyebrow, just missing her actual eye. A pine fragment filled road rash covered the left side of her face, with flesh hanging loosely from the bone.

It caught the attention of several of the other girls. The brutal wipeout was an ideal distraction for Regina to breeze through and score the first five points of the bout. Victoria reached up and grabbed the top, thicker end of the splinter, which was nearly an inch and half thick and was sticking up just above her scalp. She ripped it out of her face with a scream that echoed throughout the building. The vampire's shadowy, dark crimson blood was pouring from her face, down her shirt, and spilling onto the ground around her. Victoria let out an animalistic scream as she tossed the wooden shard to the ground and reentered the track, beginning to skate again. Normally, that would've been something that would require medical attention. But there was nothing normal about this.

Lizzy pulled herself up from the floor, covered in Victoria's blood—possibly even mixed with the blood that had been drained from her sister. Her hand was surely broken. Victoria's skate had caught it on the way down. Her arm stung, raw from the floor, but more than that she was ignoring her knee, which was throbbing. She was forcing herself to keep skating. She had just pissed off a vampire. Now it was certain for Lizzy. It was skate or die.

Chapter Thirty-Two
Kill Them All

Grayson, the ever vigilant spectator, was watching all of this happen as he finally cut through enough of the ropes keeping him bound. Flexing the muscles in his arms and chest to force the fibers in the last bit of connecting rope to shred, he struggled against the restraint. His muscles were like jelly as he tried to shake it out. His wrists were raw and his fingertips were bloody from the razor blade, but he was free. Well, he had his arms free. He reached down and started untying the ropes around his ankles and legs that kept him strapped to the chair. He did his best to ignore the ever-present stinging from the coarse fibers of the rope ripping into his gashed fingers.

Grayson freed himself and looked over to the area where the Hunny Bees had been sitting. He could see his backpack next to Orbache, who was standing up and screaming encouragement at the girls. Grayson couldn't get his attention without calling attention to himself and being seen by the vampires, so Grayson improvised. He turned his attention to Tabby. Through the discomfort, he quickly worked his way through her ropes. She was only tied up enough to support her bodyweight—there was no risk of Tabitha escaping in her current, diminished state. As he untied the top ropes, she slid off the pole and into his arms. She felt lifeless and limp. Literal dead weight. He adjusted her position and, with the help of her own body weight, threw her over his shoulder.

Grayson turned in time to see Madeline on the sideline, putting her index finger up to her mouth and pricking it on her fang. She rubbed and pushed at the puncture, waiting for the blood to pool, then she skated back onto the track, tagging out with another girl. Madeline skated fast and with purpose, coming up right behind Lizzy. She took her bloody finger and ran it down the back of Lizzy's arm, leaving a small, but a very visible mark. A movement and touch that went completely unnoticed by Lizzy.

Grayson realized that they had just marked her. He had seen it in bouts before, usually done with masking tape or cut up post-it notes. It designated the girl to hit, and a lot of times, this was personal in nature.

This time it was killing the gatekeeper to get to the queen. Lizzy was the new target—get rid of her, get to Regina.

Regina had now managed to accrue ten points compared to Bambi's three. Against all odds, the girls were actually winning. It was just what they had hoped for, but it was also what Grayson feared. They were marking them. The vampires planned to take them out one by one until there were none. Ten little monkeys jumping on the bed. One fell off, now they're all dead.

They were never going to let them live. Victoria saw the tagging and acknowledged it, signaling the others with a nod. This one was hers. Victoria had a score to settle. She took out her mouth guard and was coming up behind Lizzy quickly. Grayson had Tabby over his shoulder. He could never make it to her in time. He was out of time. He had no choice but to blow his cover.

"Twenty-eight!" he yelled. "Behind you!" His scream rang out across the room.

In one fluid movement, Lizzy grabbed the wooden stake she had rolled in the waist of her shorts and turned around, sending the dagger into the chest of Victoria, whose open, fang-bearing mouth marked the immediate change in her demeanor. A look of shock and horror rushed over her face as she looked down, slowing and coming to a screeching halt as she fell to her knees, like a marionette puppet whose strings had been cut. Lizzy spun out from the centrifugal force and wrestled herself to a stop, nearly as stunned as Victoria herself. Victoria grabbed feebly at the stub of the wood that remained protruding out of her chest. She scratched at it numbly like a bug bite. Lizzy caught her composure and got over the shock, remembering her rage.

"That's for my sister," she said as she watched the life, or whatever power kept Victoria animated, liberate its weight from her eyes.

Victoria fell forward on the track. Regina swung around them, not stopping, ignoring everything but the timer as it ticked down lower and lower. She could actually win this. Bambi was hot on her tail, screaming at the rest of the girls who were staring at the fallen skater. Their fallen sister.

"Keep playing! Keep playing!" she was screaming, crying out. She was crazed. Bambi was losing, and Bambi didn't lose.

The other girls seated on the bench now realized that Grayson was free and had Tabby with him. They quickly took off in his direction. Grayson was in trouble, and he knew it. He made a split second decision. Time and circumstance offered him no other options. He looked at Tabby.

"I am so sorry, please forgive me," he said as he rolled her down the stack to the hard floor with a thud. He ran down after her, using the momentum from the steep incline to jump over the half wall. He stumbled only briefly and started running towards Orbache, who now realized what was going on and was running to meet him with the backpack. Orbache reached in and grabbed two of the small bottles of lighter fluid, tossing them to him. Grayson turned and ripped the caps off the top of them, coating his assailants in the flammable liquid as they approached. Orbache struck a match mid-run and tossed it into the stream of liquid. It was a parlor trick he had done at barbecues for years. The liquid fire was ablaze and engulfed six of the vampires coming after them in a literal line of fire. They screamed as the flames consumed them, writhing in torment as they dropped to the floor, the melted plastic and rubber from the helmets and pads dripping off and creating flaming puddles on the ground.

Bambi slowed to a roll, watching in horror. She had now lost over half a dozen of her hand-picked minions. She stopped mid-skate, turning to throw her hands out, like wings at her sides.

"Fuck it," she uttered, spitting her mouth guard to the floor and baring her fangs.

"KILL THEM ALL!" she screamed at the top of her lungs. "Except Regina. She's mine!" She looked around the track, hellbent on laying eyes on her soon-to-be victim.

A chaotic free for all broke out almost immediately. Blood began flying. Madeline headed straight for Lizzy, who had taken out her lover, Victoria. Lizzy started trying to skate away, but Victoria leapt to the ground and caught her ankle, sending her tumbling.

Madeline was crawling up towards her, fangs bared, hissing through tears like a starved beast coming out of hibernation, ready for vengeance. Evening the score for her fallen partner and comrade.

Lizzy tried desperately to kick Madeline away, but she could not be stopped. Lizzy thought about her child, her husband, her parents, and her sister, who she would surely see again in the afterlife soon. Her life was flashing before her eyes, when Orbache came running up from the right. Gripping a long piece of metal rebar with both hands like a medieval knight, he plunged it through Madeline's back. The rebar came ripping back out through the front of her chest, connecting with the floor as she tried to crawl towards Lizzy. The rebar had caught Lizzy's leg leaving an open gash as it came out the other side of Madeline's chest and thudded against the wood floor. Madeline rocked and slid down the rest of the length of the rebar. Her body was already lifeless by the time she reached the floor.

Lizzy looked behind Orbache and saw an all-out battle raging between the girls. She scanned the area and couldn't find Regina. Or Bambi.

Regina had fallen in all the commotion and scrambled along the ground, backing herself into a corner. Trapped like an animal, she could only watch as Bambi rolled slowly towards her, towering above Regina while she struggled to find a way out or gain her footing to get off the floor.

Regina wasn't even sure how she had ended up on the ground. Perhaps she had stumbled over a body—there were so many of them now. Vampire and human alike, she had blood in her eyes. She was trying to wipe them clean, but the only sight in front of her was her attacker, the girl who intended to kill her, and Regina was not eager to see her demise clearly. Bambi pulled her helmet off, and it hit the floor with a thud.

"I just want you to know that I'm going to enjoy this," Bambi said, rolling towards her.

"Not as much as you think," Regina said, ramming her skate into Bambi's ankle, sending her face-first into the floor right beside her, just a few inches from her. Regina scrambled out of the corner, trying to get back on her feet. Bambi was clawing at her, ripping runs in her already damaged tights. She could buy new tights, but she would have to be alive to enjoy them. Regina kept fighting her way to her feet. She was offered some hope when she saw Veronica in the center of the room, fighting off one of the girls, holding her own. She could do it, too. Regina turned and saw Bambi skating up behind her fast. Regina had hoped she'd broken the bitch, but it seemed she'd had no luck there.

Regina reached to grab the stake hidden in her wrist guard, but it was gone. They were both gone. She was immediately riddled with white hot panic all over her body. They must have fallen out somewhere in the scuffle. Regina was empty-handed. It was all over—she would be caught and killed. She was defenseless. Regina scanned the floor around her, and that's when she spotted it. On the floor wedged against the wall was a bloody fucking miracle. Regina reached down mid-skate and picked up the wooden splinter that had found its way through Victoria's face. Veronica saw it, smiled and nodded in Regina's direction, and turned to punch her adversary in the face, busting her nose.

Veronica skated a game of chicken with Regina and Bambi, rushing at Regina head on. She then veered off only inches and held out her arm, hand clenched tight. Regina grabbed Veronica's fist and forearm, using the added momentum and force to whip around. The move slung her in a tight, concise loop, expertly executed and controlled by Regina. It sent her with precision exactly where she needed to be. She came up right behind Bambi and grabbed her around the neck, choking her with the crook of her arm and desperately trying to avoid her teeth. Regina's other arm hovered above Bambi's chest with the makeshift wooden stake that was already covered in the blood of her dead, parasitic follower, pressing gently against her skin.

Bambi realized her demise was close at hand. Her blood-drenched, glistening demise. She was caught. It all happened too fast for her to fathom it. Mortals shouldn't move that fast, but those gifted with immortality often underestimate the will to survive.

As Regina held her tight, Bambi dug her fingernails into her arm, drawing blood to the surface and spilling out of the wounds. She was trying to get away. She was struggling, but she was still strong.

Regina wasted no more time. She would not give her the satisfaction of letting her make it out of here alive.

Regina whispered in her ear—the last words Bambi would ever hear. "Before I send you back to hell where you came from, I want you to know two things," Regina said, out of breath. "Number one, Grayson is mine." Bambi tried to look back at her. For the first time in her afterlife, she was experiencing real fear. Regina sent the final nail in the coffin. "Number two, I just kicked your ass at roller derby."

Bambi started to squirm, but before she could make another ploy at escape, Regina sent the splinter deep into Bambi's chest. Bambi looked up at Regina, sliding to the floor. Their eyes met. Fear consumed her. Desperation and uncertainty of what was after the afterlife. Bambi lay flat on the floor, blood dampening her shirt as it gushed from her chest. She reached and clawed, like a cat reaching for floating lint in the air. Her fingers began to curl and rigor together. Regina stared down at her, unable to take her eyes off her, burdened by the terrified eyes that looked back at her. Regina was shaking from the rush of adrenaline as she watched Bambi take her last shallow, stuttered breath. Despite the grotesque scene, a sense of relief flooded over her body. She had killed her.

Regina had done it.

The ease was short-lived. Regina turned as the rest of the vampires sensed that their leader was gone. An invisible bond had been broken. They scurried away from the battle and made their way towards the doors like roaches in the night when the lights flicked on. With their master dead, they were weak and vulnerable. The buzzer had been sounding the end of the match for minutes now, no one at all concerned about turning off the annoying blaring sound. No one had even heard it amid the cacophony of battle. Regina was looking for Veronica. They had done it. They had won.

Then she saw her.

Veronica was on the ground in a pool of blood. She wasn't moving. One of last remaining vampires hurried away from her body, leaving her alone in an orange glow that was now illuminating the building. Sweat poured from Regina's face mixing with blood.

"NO!"

Regina screamed and tried to run over to Veronica, forgetting she was wearing skates. She stumbled and fell to the ground, crawling over to her and kicking her skates off as she made her way over. Regina reached her friend's body lying in a pool of blood. She saw her breathe and knelt over her. Her eyes were open. Veronica looked up at Regina, turning over to face her.

She was alive.

Regina was crying and smiling, relieved that she was alive. "We did it!" Regina said through her happy tears. Veronica slowly moved her blood-covered hand away from her neck—the source of blood.

"I was bitten," Veronica said, her hands shaking, tears pooling in her eyes.

"No, no, no," Regina pleaded, beginning to cry like a small child. "But we won, we won." She buried her head in her hands.

"My hands feel like they are asleep," Veronica observed. "Regina, they're cold," she said through tears. Regina scooted over to her and picked her up, resting her in her lap. She saw the same look of fear and uncertainty that she had seen in Bambi's eyes.

It was too late for Veronica—the metamorphosis was imminent. The virus or parasite or whatever it was launched an attack on every cell of her body. Her blood was no longer her own. The sharpness in her bones crept from her fingers. It was a chill she could not shake. It made its way up her arm and into her chest. Veronica began convulsing and slid out of Regina's lap.

Grayson and Orbache came running over, with Tabby draped over Grayson's shoulder. It was at that moment that Regina realized the entire building was on fire, filling with smoke. While the fight had been going on, while she had ended Bambi's life, Grayson and Orbache had set the world around her on fire. That was his secret plan, to burn the evidence. To burn down the house of the dead.

"We have to go!" he was screaming at her. "We have to get out of here now, Regina!" It was angrier than he had intended, but the urgency was real. All she heard was silence. She saw his lips moving, but the orange glow around them consumed the words. The building was getting hot—much longer, and they may not make it out alive.

"We have to go now!" he screamed again.

"She was bitten!" Regina choked out, breaking into tears again.

"Get her out of here, we can't let her burn," Grayson replied, hoping to make sense of everything outside, away from the flames.

Veronica lay on the floor convulsing. Regina looked at her. "I can't, I can't." Regina was shaking, too overcome with emotions and tears to do anything. She threw herself onto the floor sobbing, shutting down.

Orbache grabbed Veronica under the arms and began dragging her across the floor to the exit as she seized and hissed. With Tabby over his shoulder, Grayson reached his free arm and bent down as far as he could without losing his balance, grabbing Regina's shoulder and moving down to her arm to pull her up. He looked at her tear-filled eyes.

"Baby, we have to go," he told her softly.

How she heard him over the building's destruction, she would never know. But she knew he was right. She hadn't survived all of this to die now. She got to her feet, and they ran to the door as the room was bathed in flames, shrieks and screams escaping from a few of the injured vampires who had not been able to make it out. The birds in the rafters flew out several of the windows that had busted out from the heat of the fire.

They exited the burning building together. Falling to the dock as they got out the door, they scrambled and moved far from the building, dragging Tabitha as far as they could get before they had to catch their breath.

Once out of the building, safely escaped and distanced from the Mother Suckers and the fire, they looked back at the glowing blaze.

"It's like we just escaped hell," Orbache said.

Grayson looked down at Veronica, becoming pale and cold right before their eyes. "Not all of us," Grayson said solemnly.

Chapter Thirty-Three
Already Dead

Grayson pulled his stake from the back belt loops of his pants and stood over Veronica. Looking down at his friend, knowing what had to be done. Finally able to step up and do the right thing, no matter the personal attachment.

Regina screamed and threw herself over Veronica's body. "No! Are you crazy?!" Regina was beside herself with grief. How could Grayson do this? She was still Veronica—her body wasn't even cold yet. How could he be so heartless?

"Regina, she's one of them now," he said, his tone matter of fact.

Grayson was anything but heartless. It was killing him inside, but he knew that very soon, Veronica would become a vampire. It was going to happen, and the only way to stop her was to kill her. Set her free from the curse. More than anything, he didn't want to have to see Veronica suffer the lifeless movement through existence as a vampire.

"She's my best friend," Regina said, wrapping her arms around Veronica and pulling her up to her chest. "You can't kill her."

"She's already dead," Grayson said coldly.

"What if we can fix her? What if there is a cure?" Regina bargained wildly. "We don't know anything about this. Maybe we can fix her." On her knees, Regina moved to look at him, pleading. "She won't be like them. She is still Veronica. She won't be like them, I swear she won't. I *know* she won't," Regina said, bawling, trying desperately to convince Grayson as much as she was trying to convince herself.

Several of the other girls started walking over. Orbache stepped in, cutting them off before they could see anything.

"She'll be alright. It's kind of nasty though," he said. "You guys get home, someone is bound to have seen the fire by now. We all need to get out of here and get her to an emergency room. Regina will call everyone in the next couple of days to check in," he told them. They listened, not willing or able to argue, and began heading out towards the gates, leaving the small group there on the docks in the cold, icy night air, warmed only by the heat radiating from the warehouse fire.

Veronica clung to the last shreds of her former life, spending her last seconds amongst the living, soon to be a member of the undead.

"Wait!" Regina cried, realizing Tabby was still on the ground behind her. Grayson picked Tabitha back up and ran to catch up with the girls, passing her off to Lizzy, who was now favoring her knee, no longer able to ignore the pain. "Get her to a hospital, quick!"

Lizzy nodded. "Headed that way anyway," she said with a half smile.

Gryason walked back over and stopped short next to Orbache, out of Regina's earshot, still cradling Veronica's body.

"Hey, whatever we are going to do, we need to do it now," Orbache said with urgency. "Someone has probably seen the fire by now. We need to get out of here."

Grayson walked over to Regina, choking up a little as he tossed the stake on the ground next to Veronica's body. "It's your call."

Regina grabbed the stake angrily and tossed it into the bushes.

"Help me get her out of here," Regina spat.

"Even if she is still Veronica, she will have to drink blood to survive, Regina," Orbache said, kneeling down next to the two of them. His eyes were compassionate—he had genuinely come to care for Veronica over the past few days. "Are you sure she's prepared for that?"

"I don't care," Regina commanded. "We'll figure it out. Just help me get her out of here."

Epilogue

The cold air fogged up the window of the little coffee shop with condensation, blurring the colorful lights lining the frame of the window. Their little bulbs sparkled and glistened—their colors, warm and homey.

This is not how Regina had imagined spending her first Christmas Eve with Grayson as husband and wife. Other newlyweds would be spending the evening sitting in front of a warm fire, sipping hot chocolate. Maybe she would have been getting things prepared for the next day's meal. *Sweet potato casserole,* she nodded to herself. That was all if her life had not brought her here.

She crossed her arms, trying to knock off the chill from the icy street outside. They had arrived a few minutes early for a meeting.

Regina rocked in her seat a little and glanced around the tiny cafe. She had a bright red scarf wrapped around her neck, tucked into a charcoal wool peacoat. The picture of west coast winter sophistication. They would be spending their first Christmas together in Seattle. Regina looked over at her husband, who was making pleasantries with a sad and dull-looking barista behind the counter. Mousy brown hair, mismatched blouse and cardigan. Seattle grunge was alive and well apparently. Grayson turned away from the counter with two oversized mugs in his hands, returned to the table and set them down. Grayson took a seat from her, looking at her and leaning in.

"Just so we're both clear, you know this is a set-up, right?" Grayson asked, looking at her over a pair of thick black-rimmed, square-framed glasses.

Regina took a sip of her drink and licked her lips, smiling and nodding in response.

The green wooden door swung open, ringing the little brass bell at the top. A taller gentleman in a grey, ill-fitting suit and carrying a briefcase entered. He was thin, with an unevenly blended coat of tinted foundation on his face and hands.

Grayson and Regina both shot the other a glance.

Rookie mistake, Regina thought.

As they suspected, their client tonight had set them up. It was happening more often, but it was an expected danger in what they did.

"Regina?" the man asked, looking at her.

She was the only woman in the entire place other than the barista. *Who else would it be?* she thought.

Regina smiled politely and stood up to shake the man's hand, when he lunged at her neck and tried to dig his teeth into her flesh, only to be met with a metal thud. He whipped his head back in pain, grabbing his mouth. Regina pulled the end of her scarf and revealed a custom metallic choker that ran the entire length of her neck. His eyes were wide, fear shooting through his body. He had failed his mission and was now surely dead.

"Think again, bloodsucker," Regina said as she reached into her coat, pulling out a dagger and sending it through the thin white dress shirt into the man's chest. He fell out onto the floor, and Regina looked back over at Grayson.

"Really? Did they think some poorly applied makeup was going to fool us?" Regina wondered, sort of offended that her assassin thought so little of her. She picked up her scarf and went to sit back down, annoyed.

The mousy haired girl at the cash register came leaping over the counter, fangs at the ready. Grayson jumped up and grabbed the empty chair between him and Regina, hitting her with it like she had been pitched to him. The chair shattered. He took the broken leg and sent it through her chest, ending her miserable existence before she was even able to get up off the ornately tiled floor.

"Oh," Regina said, a little surprised. Looking down at her, then back up at Grayson smoothing out his navy coat with his hands. "Did you know about the waitress?" she asked.

"Yeah, I sort of figured. The coffee sucked," Grayson replied with a smile.

"Grayson, please do not speak ill of the dead," Regina said, barely getting it out of her mouth before laughing.

Grayson chuckled and walked over to the man lying on the coffee shop floor, flipping him over and taking his wallet out of his back pocket. He pocketed the cash, dropping the now empty wallet back on the assassin's corpse. He looked back at Regina, who was silently judging him with questioning disbelief, waiting for an explanation for his thievery.

"What? He hired us for a job, the least we could do is get paid," Grayson said, pleading his case. "I don't think that check is going to clear now."

"I didn't say a word," Regina said as she stepped over the dead vampire's body, heading to the door. Grayson took another sip of his poorly brewed coffee and followed her back out into the cold.

In the two years that had passed since the derby bout, Regina and Grayson had left everything they had once known behind. Orbache had stayed in town to run the rink, promising to keep it open no matter what.

Grayson had told Orbache about their plan to leave and hunt down the west coast vampires on the eve of his and Regina's wedding. Grayson asked his best man to come with him, but Orbache had refused, telling Grayson that someone had to stay home—to remember what home was and make sure the others never forgot. While that sentiment was genuine, Orbache had also started a fairly serious relationship with a recently separated Lizzy. He didn't want to risk messing that up.

Following the bout, a friendship had developed between the two of them. She had baked him an apple pie. She said it was a thank you gesture for saving her life. And when her husband left her, the friendship had developed into something more. Orbache had finally found something he was passionate about. Grayson understood. As much as he wanted his best friend out there on the battlefield with him, he understood.

"The day you come back for good—and that day will come, my friend—it'll be here, waiting for you," Orbache had told Grayson about the rink the night before he and Regina left. That night seemed like a different lifetime to Grayson now. He still had hope of one day going back home, back to the rink, starting a family with Regina, and living the life that they had once planned for themselves. However, with every day that passed, the vision slipped further and further away. He and Regina had started a war.

Regina had been the first person to intentionally kill a vampire in over sixty years. She had become a legend. A symbol for human uprising against the shadows. Families of victims were now contacting her—she and Grayson had become contract killers.

They had been in the Pacific Northwest for nearly eight weeks now, chasing down a large, semi-nomadic, and very dangerous vampire population. To Regina's family and everyone else, they were taking an extended honeymoon. Grayson had fallen into some money with a scratch off lottery ticket. It was the party line.

But really they were trailing a community of vampires that Veronica had been able to immerse herself in. She had found a way to make her condition of use to the cause. At least, as far as she let on—she seemed to have no qualms about being a part of a militia to destroy her own newfound species. It was a species she despised anyway. She was a self-hating vampire.

Veronica had almost died the first weeks after being turned. She refused to eat. She adamantly refused to feed on the living. On several occasions, she sat outside and waited for the sunrise, hoping for it to end her life. Regina had stopped her each time and convinced her that whatever her life was now, it was worth living. A well-timed news story had given Veronica a new purpose. A way for her to survive.

A local news station had done a kick-you-in-the-gut human interest piece on mercy killings. A nurse was being tried for the murder of her patient, but the nurse claimed it was a mercy killing.

The segment had interviewed several nursing home residents including an elderly woman suffering from an inoperable and rapidly growing brain tumor. She was in tears during the story. In addition to excruciating pain, the tumor was chipping away at her memories. She said it broke her heart to be forced to have her adult daughter, who she barely recognized anymore, have to remind her of her grandchildren's names. She insisted that no child should have to ask their grandmother, "Why don't you remember me?" It wasn't fair that she was forgetting everything she had ever known and loved. She said very plainly that she was of sound enough mind to know that death was a better alternative than this shell of a life.

It was a hot button topic for sure, and the news was probably just looking for a ratings boost, but for Veronica, it was a second chance. Veronica recognized the sign of the assisted living facility that the elderly woman was living at. Weakly getting up from the bed where she was buried under countless blankets and heating pads, trying desperately to rid herself of the cold in her bones that never faded, Veronica walked through the snowy night and straight to the facility. She walked into the building without incident and found the old woman's room.

Eloise was awake, sitting on the side of her bed and staring into the nothingness of night. She looked up and saw Veronica standing in her doorway, ghostly pale and wearing a white nightgown, bathed in the cool blue light drifting down the hall from the nurses' station.

"Are you an angel?" the frail woman asked with the utmost sincerity. "Are you here to take me to heaven?"

Veronica's eyes filled with tears as she smiled and nodded. "Yes, if that's what you want," Veronica told her sweetly.

The old woman clutched her chest, smiled, and eagerly laid down on the bed with her eyes. She looked like she was practicing a pose for her coffin.

Veronica took a deep breath and walked over to her, leaning in and digging her teeth deep into the woman's neck. Eloise flinched slightly, still smiling, and then was still. Blood began pouring from the wounds and despite her automatic gag reflex, some sort of muscle instinct kicked in. Veronica fed. She dehydrated the woman's body of every last drop of fluid. As she drank, her body warmed. Veronica was able to feel the cold tile floor under her bare feet. It was the first time she had felt alive in weeks. She understood the need, the craving for blood now.

It made her feel alive.

And she had now found a way of using her curse for good. Veronica would be an angel of mercy. And it would keep her alive.

Not everyone had come out of the events of the bout as fortunate. Tabitha was hospitalized for weeks. Initially, she was treated for severe dehydration, but once she came to and began telling the authorities the wild story about vampires and the derby bout, they had moved her to a psychiatric facility for observation and treatment.

Two months after Tabby was released from the state's mental health facility, she vanished. She went off the grid, changed her name, got rid of her cell phone, left school, and disappeared into the night. She left nothing but a note that said, "Please don't find me."

No one had heard from her in over a year. Regina had gotten a birthday text from an unknown number. She pretended it was her—she hoped that it was Tabby. She hoped it meant that she was okay and that she was happy.

It was impossible to forget what happened, but Regina hoped that Tabby was able to lead a normal life somewhere else. Take advantage of a fresh start Regina knew she herself would never be afforded. Somewhere without vampires. There was no way of knowing. But Regina prayed that her old friend was doing well. Her prayers were often the only respite from the gnawing guilt Regina felt. The more quiet the night, the louder the thought. *It's my fault she is gone.*

Regina sat up in the hotel room bed and flipped through channels on the TV, hoping to find reruns of something upbeat from the nineties. So far, her search was unsuccessful, and she finally clicked the television off. Grayson had already gone to sleep next to her. She kissed his bare shoulder before pulling the thin blanket up over it.

She reached over and grabbed her laptop from the bedside table, using the hotel's sluggish Wi-Fi to pull up her email. Every day there were more and more emails. Sightings, suspicions, families needing answers. Wondering and hoping for closure.

Was it vampires? Was it vampires that had taken their loved ones from them?

She knew that she and Grayson really had no choice—they had to do this. They knew too much to turn a blind eye. They both knew in their hearts that they were meant for something more. Humanity needed someone to believe in when the things that go bump in the night turned out to be real.

And they were good at it. Now, they blurred the lines of the hunter and the hunted. And hoped to even out the score for the living.

Vampires beware.

ABOUT THE AUTHOR

Josh Blackmon began his writing career in newspapers and magazines, with his writing featured in regional and national publications. He currently works at a marketing company in north Florida, where he lives with his wife and daughter.

Josh has a passion for writing and the paranormal.

ROLLER DERBY VAMPIRE GIRL

ROLLER DERBY VAMPIRE GIRL

Made in the USA
Columbia, SC
21 December 2020